'Are you ⸻ **y no room f** ⸻

Natasha said ⸻ ⸻ surplus to requirements. No question.'

He looked down at her thoughtfully, almost pityingly. For a moment she almost thought he was going to pat her on the head. Her eyes dared him to try.

But he did something even more unsettling. He touched her lower lip with a caress. Natasha flinched as if she had scalded herself. The little touch was somehow more intimate than a kiss.

He gave a soft laugh that nobody but the two of them could have heard.

'It would take me one night to change your mind,' he murmured, his breath stirring the hair that curled round her ear. 'Just—one—night.'

Natasha gasped. She sought vainly for a crushing retort.

But it was too late. He was gone.

Born in London, **Sophie Weston** is a traveller by nature, who started writing when she was five. She wrote her first romance recovering from illness, thinking her travelling was over. She was wrong, but she enjoyed it so much that she has carried on. These days she lives in the heart of the city, with two demanding cats and a cherry tree—and travels the world looking for settings for her stories.

Recent titles by the same author:

THE DUKE'S PROPOSAL

IN THE ARMS OF
THE SHEIKH

BY
SOPHIE WESTON

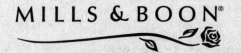

MILLS & BOON®

All the characters in this book have no existence outside the imagination
of the author, and have no relation whatsoever to anyone bearing the
same name or names. They are not even distantly inspired by any
individual known or unknown to the author, and all the incidents are
pure invention.

First published in Great Britain 2005
Harlequin Mills & Boon Limited,
Eton House, 18-24 Paradise Road, Richmond, Surrey TW9 1SR

© Sophie Weston 2005

ISBN 0 263 84274 6

Set in Times Roman 10 on 11 pt.
02-1205-55701

Printed and bound in Spain
by Litografia Rosés, S.A., Barcelona

CHAPTER ONE

NEW YORK is paradise for insomniacs, thought Natasha Lambert. It never sleeps. Let's hear it for New York!

She pressed her nose against the window of her hotel room and looked down twenty storeys. The November sky was as black as midnight. It was five in the morning. But cars' headlights still swooped along the rain soaked street and there were people on the sidewalk.

Who were they? People going to work? People coming in from all-night clubbing? Natasha could see a couple emerging from the awning of the hotel, while a porter put a mountain of baggage in their cab.

A couple... In spite of the hotel's admirable central heating, she found she was shivering. Stop that, she told herself.

Quickly, she went back to the high-concept executive desk that was the reason she had booked this luxury suite in the first place. Not that she looked like a high-concept executive at the moment, thought Natasha, grinning. Not in her sweats and beloved furry slippers with cat faces.

Her laptop stood open in a pool of light. Natasha sat down at it and wriggled her toes in their comforting fur, debating what colour to turn her presentation slides.

Blue? Too cold. Red? Too aggressive.

Just like me, she thought wryly. Her last boyfriend had delivered a comprehensive character analysis before they had stopped seeing each other. Heartless, he'd called her. It had driven him mad when she'd cheerfully agreed with him.

'It's not a compliment,' he yelled.

'Maybe not to you. I've worked hard to get like this.'

That was when he left, fuming.

Now the phone rang. Not taking her eyes off the screen, Natasha scooped it up.

'Yup?'

'Can I leave a message for Natasha Lambert, please?'

Natasha grinned. 'It's me,' she said ungrammatically. 'Hi, Izzy.'

There was an anguished screech. 'Oh, *no*.'

Natasha's grin widened. Izzy Dare was her very best friend.

'Flattering,' she remarked. 'Aren't you talking to me any more, Izzy? What have I done?'

But Izzy was too full of remorse to laugh. 'I was trying to leave a message with the desk clerk. I never meant to wake you up.'

'You didn't.'

Natasha swirled a pie chart round on the screen. Both red *and* blue maybe? After all, cold and aggressive were often an advantage in business. Heartless, she might be, but she was very successful.

It was a long time since she had cared what people said about her. Anything was fine, as long as they also said she got the job done. And they did.

She stopped playing with her pie chart. 'What can I do for you, Izzy?'

But Izzy was still worried. 'You're sure I didn't wake you? But I thought New York was five hours behind London. What on earth is the time there?'

Natasha detached her eyes from the screen and cast a rapid look at her discreetly expensive platinum watch.

'Just after five.'

'And you're up?' Izzy was horrified.

'Lambert Research never sleeps,' said Natasha smugly.

'But why?'

'Breakfast meeting with the Head Honcho. They slipped it in at the last moment, so I'm reworking the presentation.'

'Is he nice?' said Izzy, temporarily sidetracked.

'Who?'

'The Head Honcho.'

Natasha choked at the thought. 'David Frankel is a short, fat workaholic with a nasty sideline in groping if you let him get too close,' she announced. 'He's also focused as a needle.'

'Sounds horrid.'

'That's why he's Head Honcho,' said Natasha peacefully. 'Powerful men *are* horrid. It's part of their job description.'

Izzy protested.

Natasha was indifferent. 'No sweat. I work with powerful men all the time. They cause a lot of work and I wouldn't want to date one. But apart from that, they're fine. Tell me what you want.'

Izzy sounded uncomfortable. 'About the weekend—'

'Oh, *yes*. I'm really, really looking forward to it. A girls' getaway is just what I need. Especially after the week I've had.'

There was a microsecond's pause, which would have been perceptible if Natasha hadn't been tapping away adjusting the pie chart again.

This time she made it change to lime-green. The screen pulsed with virulent colour. Natasha put her head on one side. Young and exciting? Or too frivolous?

'So what about the weekend?'

'There's been a change of plan.'

Natasha sighed. 'That's a shame. Okay, let's take a rain check.'

'No, not that sort of change. A—er—different venue.'

'Okay,' said Natasha without much interest. 'Where?'

'Well…' Izzy sounded uncharacteristically embarrassed '…it's a private house now. I've sort of borrowed it.'

'Fine. Give me the address.'

Izzy did. 'And there's something else—'

At last Izzy's hesitation got through. Natasha stopped playing with the mouse. 'Okay, Izzy. Spit it out. What's the problem? The place is falling down? There's no central heating? It's so deep in the country, I'll have to hire a helicopter to get there?'

'You would too, wouldn't you?' Izzy sounded odd.

'Whatever it takes,' said Natasha briskly. 'All for one and one for all. You're my best friend and I haven't seen you for six

months.' Her fingers twitched. She left the mouse where it was.
But it was an effort. 'Am I going to have to find me a pilot?'

'No. By car, it's an hour tops from the airport.'

'Then there isn't a problem.'

'Okay, get back to your work, and I'll see you tomorrow.
You're still on the overnight flight?'

'Yup.'

'That's good. Gives us the whole day to talk before the others
get here.'

Natasha frowned. She turned her back on her laptop. This
sounded serious. 'You in trouble, Izzy?'

Her friend gave the ghost of a laugh. 'No, no, it's just that—'
Izzy stopped. Then she went on in a high, unnatural voice,
'Serenata Place is a bit difficult to find.' It was as if she wanted
to say something else and couldn't screw her courage up. 'I'll
email you a map,' she said with desperate brightness.

Natasha's frown deepened. She had never heard Izzy sound
like that before. Well, not since—

She pulled her mind away from the dark memories. The bad
time was three years past. Gone. She and Izzy had got out of
the jungle alive and well and so had everyone else. All was well
that ended well, in fact. The nightmares would go too, in time.

But that didn't explain why Izzy sounded so stiff and false.

She said sharply, 'What's wrong, Izzy?'

Izzy made an odd sound, half laugh, half sob.

'I'm getting married.'

'You're *what?*'

'Married,' said Izzy, gabbling. 'I know. I know. It's very sudden. You don't know him. Only he's going away and…this
weekend is our engagement party.'

Natasha frowned at the phone for a long moment. Izzy was
a practical, strong-minded woman, but she had her area of vul-
nerability. And Natasha knew exactly where it was. Izzy was at
work. She worked with her cousin Pepper in a bright, fashionable office. It was open-plan and anyone could listen to everyone's conversations. Would Izzy want to discuss everything with
her co-workers listening in? No, she would not.

'Look—I'll see you on Friday and tell you everything. Have a good flight.' Izzy rang off.

Okay, she would wait until their tête-à-tête on Friday. But then, she resolved, Izzy was going to tell, and tell *everything*.

Meanwhile, there was no point in thinking about it. Izzy's sudden marriage could go on hold for a few hours. Natasha, the professional, had a presentation to finalise.

She turned back to the laptop and, with a savage stab at the keyboard, sent her pie chart purple.

The throne room at the palace was a hotchpotch of magnificence and sheer eccentric indulgence. The Emir of Saraq sat on a French brocade chair that would have looked more at home in Versailles and waved the new arrival onto a minimalist Swedish sofa. The Emir had commissioned it personally.

'You don't command me, Grandfather,' said the new arrival, without emotion. He was tall with decided eyebrows and a great haughty beak of a nose. His stark white robe was creaseless. He did not sit down.

'You are here,' the Emir pointed out with a touch of defiance.

'For the moment.'

Their eyes clashed: the Emir's fierce; the watcher's unreadable. He had had a lot of practice at masking his feelings. He was good at it.

The Emir's gaze was the first to fall.

'Don't let's argue, Kazim. This is important.'

The placatory tone was out of character. But his grandfather was a consummate actor, thought Kazim, and as wily as a hunting falcon. He stayed watchful.

'Is this about another arranged marriage?'

The Emir's eyes flashed. But almost at once he curbed himself.

'No. I have agreed. You will decide for yourself when you marry.' It sounded as if every word were dragged from him, but he still got it out.

It was not enough. Kazim stayed implacable.

'*If* I marry,' he corrected.

The old man did not like that, either. 'If you marry,' he agreed reluctantly.

Kazim was remorseless. 'And who I marry.'

'And who you marry.' It was said through gritted teeth.

His grandson nodded slowly, like a general accepting surrender. 'I will.'

They eyed each other like duellists.

The Emir said something explosive under his breath.

Kazim decided not to hear it. Sometimes it was the only possible move in the prolonged chess game of their relationship.

'You break with every tradition and listen to nobody—but you do get things done.'

Kazim's lips twitched. 'Thank you—I think.'

The Emir stopped muttering and rearranged the fold of his white robe over his knees. He was obviously making a great effort to appear reasonable. 'I wanted to see you because there has been a warning.'

Suddenly, all Kazim's wariness dissolved in concern. 'You mean threats? Against you?'

The Emir permitted himself a thin smile. 'No. You.'

For a moment Kazim's face was wiped absolutely clear of expression. He did not answer. The atmosphere in the throne room was suddenly charged with electricity.

'So you knew,' said the Emir softly.

Kazim was disturbed. He had not meant to give so much away. The old man was too good at this. Or I'm losing my touch. Not a good thought, that. He buried his unease, professional that he was, and shrugged.

'There are always crackpots. Threats come with the territory.'

'And you're setting yourself up as a target for them,' said his grandfather with sudden anger.

Kazim sighed. This was not new. His grandfather wanted him home and safe in Saraq, not continent-hopping involved in peace talks.

The old man grunted. 'This International Reconciliation Council of yours is a great idea. Very high-minded.' He paused for his effect. 'In about fifty years' time.'

'We haven't got fifty years,' said Kazim, a touch wearily. They had had this argument before, many times; most explosively the day he'd left a year ago. He braced himself to argue the case.

But for once the Emir was not after a good argument. 'That doesn't matter.'

Kazim was astonished. 'Excuse me?'

'You've got yourself on an assassination list,' the old man told him brutally.

Kazim stood like a rock. 'Your spies are very efficient,' he said politely.

The Emir glared. 'You're very cool about it.'

Kazim shrugged again. 'I take reasonable precautions.'

'No, you don't.'

That made Kazim blink. 'What?'

'Getting rid of your security and even your servants for a whole weekend is not taking reasonable precautions,' announced the Emir.

Kazim was thunderstruck.

'Isn't that what you're going to do?'

'Invasion of privacy is an alien concept to you, isn't it?' said Kazim grimly.

'I look out for my own.'

'By keeping them under twenty-four-hour surveillance?'

The Emir ignored that. 'If it's a woman, bring her here, where you'll be safe. You can have the Sultana's Palace and all the privacy you want.'

A muscle worked in Kazim's jaw. 'It is not a woman,' he said in a goaded voice.

It took a lot to get under controlled Kazim's skin these days. For the first time in the interview the Emir grinned.

'Better if it were. You work too hard.'

They both knew that Kazim had not visited his allotted rooms in the Emir's palace for years. He had come straight from the airport to this meeting and the Emir knew that, in all probability, the private jet was being refuelled even as they spoke.

The Emir had learned the hard way that if it came to a battle of wills between them, Kazim would walk away without a backward look if he thought he was in the right. But this was more than their usual battle of wills. Suddenly he was not the Emir; he was just a man, desperately worried for his grandson's safety.

'At least keep up security at Serenata Place.' It was as close to a plea as the old autocrat could manage.

Kazim was still smouldering at the thought of being spied on. 'My arrangements to entertain my friends are my own business.'

His grandfather exploded. 'Friends! What sort of friends want to put you in danger?'

'Ordinary friends,' retorted Kazim.

'Pah!'

But there was a note of real despair in the old man's voice. Kazim paused, then sat on the sofa and leaned forward slightly.

'It is only for the weekend,' he said in a softened voice.

'Duration is irrelevant,' said the Emir. 'It would take a sniper less than a minute to kill you.' He glared at Kazim as if he hated him.

'I'll have Tom do a complete sweep before the guests arrive on Friday,' Kazim said gently. 'And I'll get the full security team in when the servants come on duty again.'

The Emir made a noise of undisguised contempt.

Kazim became noticeably less gentle. 'But I can't have my best friend's engagement party spoiled by men with headsets and professional paranoia.'

'A party! Have you even checked the guest list?'

Kazim was suddenly every inch the desert prince. 'Dominic is my friend.'

'I thought not,' said his grandfather with angry satisfaction.

Kazim unbent a little. 'Grandfather, try to understand. Dom and I go climbing together. He has held my life in his hands and I his. Of course I haven't run checks on his friends.'

'Cancel this party!'

Kazim's gaze was level. 'In my place, would you?'

He knew a lot of stories about his grandfather's youth. Courage and loyalty featured highly. So did sheer wilfulness.

He lowered his eyes. 'Everything I am I have inherited from

my illustrious forebears,' he murmured, the picture of a dutiful descendant.

The Emir narrowed his eyes. 'There's such a thing as being too clever,' he said obliquely. 'One day you'll fall flat on that smug face of yours.'

Kazim's dark eyes, so like the Emir's, lit with sudden humour. 'When that happens, I'll make sure you know immediately,' he assured his grandfather.

And took his leave.

His personal assistant was waiting for him beside the air-conditioned four-wheel drive in the palace's security yard when Kazim emerged. His angry strides made his white robe billow.

'Well?'

'The old man has a spy in my household,' said Kazim between his teeth. 'He wants me to fill Serenata Place with twenty-four-hour security. Give me the keys.'

Martin's heart sank. But he handed over the keys. Most of the time Kazim was open to reason, but these encounters with his grandfather tended to ignite his temper. He had been known to smoulder for days.

Martin fell into step beside him, shaking his head. 'This is about Dominic's weekend, right?'

'Yes.'

'Well, he has a point.'

They had reached the car. Just about to swing himself up behind the steering wheel, Kazim paused.

'Listen to me, Martin,' he said deliberately. 'I spend my public life surrounded by bodyguards and security timetables. Just once, I want to give a party like an ordinary man.'

Martin had worked for Kazim a long time. He knew when his boss was not going to change his mind.

They all did, the people who worked for Kazim. The households dreaded it; the office dealt with it; his personal staff called it Kazim in sheikh mode. It didn't happen often. But when it did, he was immoveable.

Martin sighed. 'It's your decision.'

They got into the car. Kazim started the engine, checking the Global Positioning Unit.

'If I can't trust a man I climb with, I can't trust anyone.'

Martin was sympathetic. But it was his job to remind Kazim of unwelcome truths. 'You haven't climbed with the girlfriend. Or the girlfriend's girlfriends.'

Kazim turned his head in pure astonishment. 'You think the Sons of Saraq will send some London fashionista to assassinate me?'

Martin gave a crack of laughter. 'Put like that it doesn't seem likely,' he admitted.

Kazim put the car in drive. For the first time in days, his eyes were dancing. 'All I can say is, she'd better be blonde!'

He stayed in that frivolous mood all through the flight back to London, to the despair of Martin and Tom Soltano, Kazim's American Head of Security. By the time they had been in the air an hour, Martin Page was holding onto his temper so hard it squeaked. And then Kazim said something so outrageous that he exploded.

'You *are* joking?'

Kazim raised his haughty profile from the file he was frowning through and his eyebrows rose.

'I never joke about the diary.'

It was all too nearly true. In the last crowded years, Kazim had shuttled round the world, bringing his particular brand of high intellect and measured calm to conflicts from desert to inner city. It was an important schedule and a responsible one. But it did not make for a lot of laughs.

Martin, who organised most of it, knew all about that. Now he jumped up and flung a poster sized chart down on the table in front of Kazim. It showed his appointments, day by day, for six months ahead. Martin stabbed a finger at the week Kazim had been talking about. 'Just *look*. You haven't got time.'

Kazim stayed serene, as he always did. It was one of his most irritating characteristics. 'Then I will make time.'

Martin swung round and looked at him broodingly. 'Maybe

you're so good at making peace because everyone in the room ends up hating you.'

Tom Soltano gave a choke of laughter, which he converted quickly into a cough.

Kazim said calmly, 'There is always a solution.'

But Martin was too wound up to stop. 'Look at that month. New York, Paris, Saraq, Indonesia, Turkey. You can't be certain you will even make Dominic's wedding, let alone run the show.'

Kazim smiled. He had a beautiful smile. It lit his eyes, turning the stern face to melting charm in the flick of an eyelash. That smile made women adore him. Martin regarded it with deep suspicion.

'But I am not going to run Dominic's wedding,' said Kazim mildly. 'He has asked me to be his best man. That is all. I gather I stand there holding the wedding rings. How time-consuming can it be?'

Martin stared at him, speechless. American Tom was more forthright.

'Have you *been* to an English wedding?'

Kazim al Saraq was brilliant and powerful, with an arrogantly sculpted profile and enough oil wells to mean that people generally did not argue with him. But the other two were his closest associates. They never remembered the oil wells and ignored the profile.

After a few seconds in which he tried and failed to outstare them, Kazim became ever so slightly defensive. 'An English wedding? Naturally.'

'A big one? With aunts in hats? Mothers in tears?' pressed his security adviser with feeling.

Kazim's lips twitched. 'Weddings aren't so different across cultures,' he said dryly. 'Mothers in tears are standard from Bombay to Baffin Island.'

All three men contemplated the thought. All three shuddered.

Then Tom pulled himself together. 'I guess you're right about mothers,' he admitted. 'But the British best man is unique. And it's a lot more than holding a couple of rings, believe me. I've done it.'

Martin nodded. 'Listen to the man.'

Kazim smiled reluctantly. 'Okay. Go ahead. Terrify me.'

The other two looked at each other.

'Well,' said Tom with relish. 'You're responsible for the groom. I mean *responsible*. You have to give him the party of his life. Even when he's married he supposed to look back on it as his last days of freedom. That sort of party.'

'And then you sober him up the next day and get him to church,' interjected Martin.

Kazim waved that aside. 'Dominic will be in training for his South Pole expedition. There will be no drunkenness. So no sobering up.' There was a gleam of fun that they hadn't seen for ages. 'You'll have to do better than that.'

'Okay,' said Martin. 'How's this? He'll have all his mates acting as ushers. You won't know them and half of them won't know each other, but you have to tell them what to do. And keep control of the pageboys and flower girls and bridesmaids.'

'You mean: run the show,' said Kazim, still infuriatingly calm. 'I can do that. What else do I do with my life?'

Martin cast his eyes to heaven.

Tom said kindly, 'You tell Martin and me what to do and *we* run the show.'

Martin stopped looking heavenwards. 'That is so true.'

Tom was earnest. 'Best man is a hands-on kinda thing, Kazim. I'd have to advise against it. You'd be out there as a sitting target.'

Martin nodded. 'And you wouldn't be able to wave a hand and say, "Let it be so", either. You'd have to roll up your sleeves, spit on your hands and get stuck in yourself. No one to delegate to.'

Kazim remained unmoved.

Martin almost danced with irritation. But the Princeton man stuck to his point. 'Like—you have to run the speeches at the meal after the ceremony,' he pursued. 'Hell, you have to make the worst one yourself.'

Kazim was suddenly frosty. 'I make speeches all the time.'

'Not like this,' said Martin with feeling. 'You have to tell jokes.'

For a moment Tom forgot about the threatening email in his Immediate Action folder. 'Do you know any stories about Dominic Templeton-Burke that will make a bunch of strangers laugh, Kazim?' he asked curiously.

For the first time, Kazim paled. The other two saw it with satisfaction.

'And what about bridesmaids?' added Tom, beginning to enjoy himself. 'You do know you're supposed to escort the chief bridesmaid down the aisle after the bride and groom and all the aunts say what a lovely couple you make.'

'Yup,' said Martin with relish. 'There'll be a party afterwards, right? Okay, then. You have to dance with the ugliest bridesmaid. And keep on dancing with her whenever she's on her own.'

'Make sure none of the pageboys throws up over the wedding presents,' added Tom, who had indeed been a best man several times. 'Introduce people. Keep the two mothers-in-law from each other's throats and the fathers-in-law from the brandy bottle. Send the happy couple off with a smile, having made sure that nobody vandalises their car first.'

Kazim looked appalled. But he gave an uneasy laugh. 'You're exaggerating.'

Martin shook his head. 'Not a word of a lie.'

Kazim straightened his shoulders. 'Tom did it and survived. It can't be that bad.'

The other two looked at each other again.

'Worse,' they said in unison.

They spent an enjoyable ten minutes telling him the worst wedding disasters either of them could remember.

'Don't think you can fly in, stand at the altar beside Dom for ten minutes and then fly out,' Tom warned earnestly. 'Can't be done.'

'Call him and tell him to get someone else,' said Martin, not laughing any more. 'It's the only answer.'

But Kazim's chin lifted. 'I have given Dom my word.'

'Yeah, but you weren't thinking,' began Tom.

'My *word*.'

Martin knew that was the end of it. If Kazim made a promise, then nothing would sway him. Ever.

'If I cannot do this, I am a smaller man than I should be.'

There was a little silence. The other two recognised defeat.

'You're a good man, Kazim,' said Tom, moved.

Martin was no less moved. But he was still practical. 'Frankly, my sympathies are with the ugliest bridesmaid.'

CHAPTER TWO

TO THE private relief of Kazim's advisers, there was not a blonde in sight as Dom's guests began to arrive at Serenata Place that Friday. The fiancée turned out to be a redhead with a gorgeous figure and an anxious expression.

'Big house syndrome,' said Dom affectionately as she fled upstairs to change.

Kazim was startled. 'Excuse me?'

'Izzy went into a spin when I took her home to meet my parents. Now anything resembling a portrait of an ancestor and she freaks.'

A nineteen-twenties interior decorator had covered the walls of the entrance hall of Serenata Place with Victorian hunting prints. Kazim looked at the nearest picture of scarlet-coated fat men on fatter horses thundering over a hedge.

'They're not my ancestors,' he said, revolted.

Dom grinned. 'I'll tell her. That will set her mind at rest.'

Kazim, taking hourly phone calls from a jumpy security officer, did not have a lot of time for socialising that evening. But even to him it was obvious that red-headed Izzy was more and more distracted as the guests arrived and the party started. Eventually he came out of the study to find Dom looking worried.

Kazim raised his eyebrows. 'Now what?'

'The best friend hasn't arrived,' said Dom. 'We can't announce the engagement until she gets here, apparently.'

Kazim stayed calm. 'What do you want to do?'

'Murder the woman.'

'Obviously,' said Kazim dryly. 'Failing that?'

Dom scowled at the florist's best efforts. 'Postpone everything. Announcement, champagne, fireworks, the lot. Put it all on hold until tomorrow and hope the damn woman gets here then.'

Kazim blinked. But all he said was, 'Just as well all your guests are staying for the whole weekend, then.'

'Yes, thanks to you.' Dom gave a heartfelt sigh and biffed him lightly on the upper arm. 'I've definitely got a better class of friend than Izzy has.'

Kazim was amused. 'You have met the missing friend, then?'

'Miss Hot Shot?' Dom shook his head. 'Not so far.'

'She sounds intriguing,' said Kazim politely.

Dom let out a crack of laughter. 'Not your type.'

'I thought you hadn't met her.'

'I don't have to. She's been a prize pain in the neck so far. And quite apart from that, I hear she is definitely a twenty-first-century go-getter.'

Kazim shook his head sorrowfully. 'I don't know why you would say that's not my type.'

'Because you think a woman's place is on the receiving end of roses and poetry,' said his friend. 'Just before you send them home, leaving you to get on with saving the world from itself.'

Kazim was unoffended. 'Very amusing,' he said calmly. 'But—' His phone began to beep again. He flicked it open. 'Excuse me.'

Tom's text message was unequivocal. Kazim must call him *immediately*. New information was coming in about threats to the reconciliation talks, and to Kazim in particular. Tom needed advice.

Kazim sighed. 'Sorry, Dom. Work. It never goes away entirely. I'll deal with this and catch you later.'

Dom nodded. Kazim's friends were used to such interruptions. 'I'll persuade Izzy to come down and open some bottles. We'll get the party on the road.'

'And have the firework people come back tomorrow,' Kazim reminded him.

Natasha had a bad day. First, the purple pie chart did not do the business for her. Nor did her superb presentation file. David

Frankel wanted her personal, undivided attention and he was paying the piper. There was no way he was going to let her go before he was good and ready, preferably not until she agreed to have dinner with him.

As he asked question after pointless question, she saw her chance of getting first one flight, then another disappear. Smiling hard, she excused herself and called Izzy from the ladies' cloakroom. Izzy did not answer.

Natasha left a message. 'Izzy, I'm going to be late. Powerful men and their little quirks! Sorry, love. See you as soon as I can.'

It was a repeating pattern in the frustrating hours that followed. The last flight out took off late; hit fog; was diverted… Natasha calculated time-zone differences and called and called. Izzy never once picked up her phone.

In the end it was a dark Saturday evening when Natasha's hired limousine edged its way through narrow Sussex lanes at last. The chauffeur's silence was more eloquent than a stream of complaint. They had been through a ten-house village at least three times when Natasha spied a steep single-track road to their left.

'There.'

Sulkily the chauffeur did as he was told. The heater spluttered and died.

Natasha shivered. She didn't travel in Prada, but she didn't travel in Arctic expeditionary wear either. In ten denier and handmade stilettos, her toes were slowly turning to ice.

'I hope it's not far. We're miles from anywhere.'

The chauffeur sniffed.

To their right, there were hedges and dark fields; to their left, a high laurel hedge. It was beautifully clipped.

'Looks like some sort of stately home in there,' Natasha said doubtfully. 'Hope we haven't gone wrong again.'

And then there was a signpost. 'Serenata Place. Strictly Private.'

'Friendly,' Natasha remarked.

And very, very grand. She was startled, though she did not say that aloud.

What did it matter how grand it was? she told herself robustly. She could handle grand. She could handle anything.

But as the limo turned in through high hedges and was brought to a stop by massive wrought-iron gates Natasha felt her confidence wavering, for once.

She set her teeth and did not let it show. Instead she lowered the electric window and spoke briskly into the entry camera.

'Ms Lambert for Ms Dare. I'm expected.'

There was no voice on the other end. No response at all. Just a long, sinister pause.

Then, at last, the gates swung inward. Silently.

Natasha shivered again; not entirely because of the temperature.

'Oh, great. All it needs is for Lurch the butler to come swaying out of the shadows,' she muttered, thoroughly put out.

She closed the window and sat back, looking about her. They were going through some seriously stately grounds. The drive was longer than a jumbo's runway. And then they came to the house…

'Enough turrets to turn Disney studios green with envy,' said Natasha, blankly. 'And Sleeping Beauty's forest to protect it! Why on earth didn't Izzy tell me she was borrowing a Gothic mansion?'

The chauffeur did not answer.

The limousine stopped. However sulky he felt, the chauffeur had been well trained. He extracted her compact luggage and took it up the front steps. He rang an impressive bell pull before coming back to open the door of the limousine for her. If it had still been raining he would have held an umbrella over her head.

'Thank you,' said Natasha, getting out like a princess.

She had the oddest feeling she was being watched. But the front door remained closed and the windows were dark. In spite of a porch light like a beacon, there was no sound of life.

She went up the front steps. They struck cold as ice through the soles of her fashionable pumps. Marble, she thought, resigned. Definitely the real thing. A mansion indeed.

'I suppose this really is the right place—' she began.

But the driver was making good his escape. She watched the limousine drive off through the trees and found that her heart was sinking.

Natasha took hold of herself. Was she a woman or a wimp?

'The butler probably has to fight his way out of the coffin to get to the front door,' she told herself mordantly. 'Great stuff, Izzy. A themed weekend!'

She pressed the doorbell again several times. Hard.

The feeling of being watched intensified. It was like standing in a spotlight. She tilted her head, listening…

Was that a noise…?

No, she told herself. No, not an actual noise. She could not *hear* anything but the wind in the trees. No steps on the raked gravel path. No breathing.

But something inside her knew he was there. Her blood seemed to get heavy; move more slowly. Her bones tingled.

Be careful.

Natasha swallowed. The Gothic atmosphere was really getting to her! She rang the bell again and again, heart beating hard.

Then, like a shot from a gun, there came the crackle of dry leaves underfoot.

She froze. Imagination was one thing. Instincts screaming at her to be on the alert were something totally different. Natasha had learned to trust her instincts. They had saved her life once. She whipped round.

'Who's there?'

She scoured the shadows as if each one hid a personal assassin.

The man emerged from the darkness between two huge bushes. He was not stealthy, but he walked lightly. He was tall, wearing something dark.

Natasha's first impression was that he was very professional. Professional what, she was not sure. But, a professional herself, she recognised the characteristics: tense, focused, controlled. Her

second impression, which blasted the first away like a firestorm—was total arrogance.

Natasha knew arrogance in all its forms. She worked with it
every day and, once, it had nearly cost her her life. She detested
it. On pure reflex, she went into defensive mode. Her backbone
locked and her chin came up like a fighter plane taking off.

The man looked at her. He did not say anything. The reflected
light from the porch picked up high, haughty cheekbones and
eyes that pierced. Just for the moment she thought of a jungle
cat, watchful and contained. And dangerous.

Dangerous? She fought with herself. This was a shadow of
the past, pure and simple. Nothing more. She was not going to
let paranoia get to her after all these years. She set her teeth.

'Good evening.' Her tone was pleasant—well, fairly pleasant.
It said she reserved the right to lash out if he didn't jump to
attention. Close associates would have recognised that tone.

The man from the shadows was unmoved. More, he was unimpressed.

'Yes?' It was about as welcoming as a firestorm, too.

It would have intimidated a lesser woman. Natasha was almost certain it was meant to intimidate her.

It didn't. She wasted no more time on civilities.

'I'm expected,' she said briskly.

That did not impress him either. 'And you are?'

'Ms Lambert to see Ms Dare.' It was as curt as if she were
calling at one of the big New York skyscrapers and he were a
lowly reception clerk. 'Do I have to repeat myself? I told you
on the entry phone.'

He did not like that. He stiffened.

That gave Natasha some slight satisfaction. But not enough
to compensate for standing out here in the cold November wind
in a designer suit that was definitely aimed at the indoor market.
She refused to shiver, though.

'Lambert?'

'Natasha Lambert.' She was nearly snarling. 'Ms Dare asked
me for the weekend.'

He pretended to think about it—with insulting slowness. 'That was the weekend that started last night? Or this morning at the latest?'

If it hadn't been so cold, Natasha would have told him that her travel arrangements were her own business. But she was desperate to get indoors out of the biting wind.

'I was held up.' She gritted her teeth and tried hard to sound reasonable. She couldn't quite manage apologetic.

But it did not seem that he was interested in an apology, after all.

'Why?' It shot at her like a bullet.

'My client in New York demanded an extra meeting.'

He looked at her, but it was almost as if he did not see her. He frowned.

'When was the meeting?'

A little gust of ice-fringed air sent the leaves dancing. Her interrogator did not even seem to notice. But it cut through Natasha's fashionable suit like a laser ray.

This time when she gritted her teeth it was to stop them from chattering. 'Thursday evening.'

'Why didn't you take an overnight flight?'

'They were full. Then my flight was delayed, diverted due to fog—' Natasha got her second wind. 'Look, what is this? I'm supposed to be spending the weekend with friends. Not giving a rundown of my recent diary to—to—' she looked at the height, the impassive face, the body impervious to cold, those eyes focused elsewhere, and the perfect insult leaped straight out of her childhood '—to Lurch the butler,' she finished with relish.

'*What?*'

He was looking at her now, all right. Right at her. Into her, almost.

Natasha saw him take in her beautifully cut black suit, the thin, ultra-smart New York shoes, the power blonde crop. And saw him decide he didn't like the package one bit. She began to feel better, in spite of the cold.

'I beg your pardon?' he said, very slowly and distinctly.

'You're the butler, right?' she said airily. 'I mean, someone had to press the button to open those gates. You?'

He inclined his head. It was just about agreement.

'So you have to know that I am expected,' she pointed out triumphantly. She waved a hand at the case. 'Would you take my luggage, please?'

He looked at it with—would that be astonishment?

She could not resist teasing all that glacial disapproval. 'Hey, I travel light.'

His mouth set in a thin, ferocious line. It drove two deep clefts down his cheeks.

Ouch, thought Natasha. Maybe she had gone a bit far, calling him Lurch. Maybe he was sensitive about being a butler for some reason.

'So where is Ms Dare?' she asked in a friendlier tone. 'Why can't I get a rise out of the house? Have they decamped to the movies or something?'

He didn't respond to friendliness. Hardly opening his lips, he said, 'The party is in the garden.'

'Well, thank God there's some partying going on somewhere.'

He sent her a look of acute dislike. 'You have some identification?'

'Ident—?' All desire to be friendly left Natasha abruptly. 'You've got to be joking.'

But he strode forward, quick and sudden as that jungle cat she had thought him. He ran—no, surged like a tidal wave—up the steps. In spite of herself, Natasha retreated before him. It made her spitting mad but she couldn't help herself.

She stopped just short of backing up against the studded door.

'What the hell do you think you're doing?'

He ignored that. He clicked his fingers. 'Passport. You must have a passport. If you've just flown in.'

'Of course, I've just flown in,' flashed Natasha.

'Then prove it.'

Shaking with fury as much as cold now, she fumbled all the documents out of her shoulder bag—passport, the remains of her airline ticket, the travel agent's printed itinerary.

He held them out under the porch spotlight to scrutinise them.

'What were you before you took to butlering?' Natasha's tone was poisonous. 'Customs officer? Tax inspector? Really went to your head, didn't it?'

He ignored that too. He was studying her passport.

She hated her passport photograph. It had been taken nearly ten years ago. She had not been long back from the jungle. It made her look like a student, all unkempt curls and no make-up.

'Not a very good likeness,' he commented. Was there a hint of amusement in the clipped voice?

Natasha's dislike of the man intensified by several megawatts. How dared he laugh at her? She snatched her passport back with a hand that shook.

'Satisfied?'

He shrugged. 'As long as Ms Dare recognises you.'

Natasha blinked. 'What?'

'There are forged passports.'

She made a scornful noise. 'You watch too much television.'

He gave a bark of laughter.

It was too much. Natasha fished her mobile phone out of her bag and shook it open. 'Oh, enough. I'm calling Izzy *now*…'

The little machine was torn from her hand and thrown hard across the gravel driveway.

'My phone…' It was a squeak of pure outrage.

Squeak? She was furious with herself. She should have been roaring at him like a volcano! The breathless voice did not even sound like her own. Feeble, feeble, *feeble*. Natasha hated being feeble. It hadn't happened in a long time.

'How dare you?' she choked.

He was icy. 'You don't need a phone. If it is a phone.'

He took a step forward.

Natasha felt the squashy weight of her carry-on overnight case against the back of her knees. And realised she had retreated yet again. It was too much. Simple self-respect demanded that she fight back.

She tried to kick him. It was childish, inelegant—and she was off balance. She kicked the bag instead. It fell on its side. Then slowly tumbled, corner over corner, down the steps.

'Get away from me,' she said with concentrated fury.

But he was not listening to her. He was not even looking at her any more. He was looking over his shoulder, staring at the bag as if it were alive.

It had fallen in the pool of light at the bottom of the steps.

'What are you waiting for?' said Natasha acidly. 'An explosion?'

He looked back at her then. For a moment it was as if a shutter had opened. His eyes were hard and yet somehow—resigned. Her brow creased.

At once the shutter came down, hard. 'I guess not.'

'You *did* think it would explode,' said Natasha slowly. Her anger evaporated into something a lot more complicated. Without realising it, she shivered.

He released her from that piercing inspection and stepped back.

Natasha drew a shaky breath. She was worried now. What on earth had Izzy been up to?

Abruptly, he turned away and ran down the steps to take up her overnight case. Natasha tried hard to banish the feeling that he handled it as if he had just requisitioned a consignment of dynamite.

'Come with me,' he flung over his shoulder. And set off without looking back.

Natasha caught him up on an ill lit path round the side of the house. She had recovered her sense of outrage by then.

'Tell me,' she said with deceptive affability. 'When they sacked you from the police academy, was it for being too keen?'

He did not even admit to having heard her.

He set a brisk pace that made no allowance for Manhattan footwear, uneven downhill paths or the darkness. Natasha was too proud to remind him. When she found she was lagging so far behind that the striding figure was disappearing in the darkness, she set her jaw and kicked her shoes into the bushes. And caught up with him.

He did not notice.

After that, she kept up pretty well, in the circumstances. Her

shoes, even if she ever managed to find them again, would probably be ruined, she thought wryly. To say nothing of ten-denier
woodsmoke designer hose. But that was a small price to pay for
not having to admit she needed help. And at least he was car-
rying her suitcase.

It was a big party. There must have been two dozen people
there. They laughed and talked in the flickering light of a bonfire.
The girls wore all-weather jackets; the men were mostly in thick
sweaters. Apart from the man who had met her on the doorstep,
of course. He wore a suit, with no concessions at all to the
November chill.

Natasha looked round the crowd and sighed. So much for a
girls' weekend! The comforting image of sitting on the rug in
front of a blazing fire with Izzy, a couple of mates and several
bottles of wine evaporated. It was like a lost vision of paradise.
But if this was what Izzy wanted… Natasha squared her shoulders and pinned on a wide social smile.

The bonfire was huge. It blazed cheerfully at the edge of a
small lake. The air was full of the smell of mulled wine, bar-
becued sausages and potatoes baked in their jackets.

And at last she realised what was happening. 'It's a firework
party!'

There was a shriek. 'Natasha. Natasha. I thought you'd stood
me up.' Izzy burst out of the crowd round the bonfire and
hugged her in a crushing embrace.

'Sorry. I tried to get a message through.' Natasha returned the
hug enthusiastically until she ran out of air. Gasping, she fought
her way back to oxygen. 'What on earth are you wearing, Izzy?'

Izzy grinned. 'Fur-lined waxed jacket,' she said profession-
ally. 'What the well-dressed mountaineer is wearing.'

'Why?' said Prada's best customer, honestly puzzled. 'It's lethal. I nearly choked in there. And it makes you look like a
beach ball.'

'It keeps me warm,' said Izzy unanswerably. 'I don't care
how I look. We're going to have fireworks later. People won't
be looking at me.'

Natasha groaned. 'You're hopeless. No one would think you worked in fashion.'

'And no one would think you didn't,' Izzy retorted. She looked over her friend's shoulder and smiled. 'Where did you find her, Kazim?'

'On the doorstep,' said Natasha's adversary briefly.

'Like a Christmas present,' said Izzy, beaming.

'Or a pizza you haven't ordered,' muttered Natasha.

Izzy was startled. 'What?'

But Natasha was not looking at her. She glared at the man called Kazim. 'I gather I'm so late you thought I was off your guest list.'

His eyes narrowed in the firelight. They glinted evilly. He said, 'If you had called…' He sounded like a hanging judge.

Even Izzy said apologetically, 'Actually, that's true, Tasha. When you didn't turn up last night, I thought you weren't coming.'

'But I've left message after message.'

Izzy looked guilty. 'In the excitement, I forgot to top up my phone.'

Natasha shook her head. 'So you didn't get even one of my messages? What on earth did you think I was doing?'

Izzy bit her lip. 'I suppose I just thought something more important had come up.'

Natasha was genuinely shocked. 'I'm not that rude. Am I?'

'Not rude,' said Izzy forgivingly. 'Just busy being a tycoon.'

'I'm not!'

Izzy smiled. 'How many times have you blown me out this year?'

That was horribly true. Natasha could not deny it.

'Never mind,' said Izzy blithely. 'You're here now. That's all that matters.'

Even in the fitful light of the bonfire, it was clear that Kazim Whoever-he-was did not agree. Natasha's guilty conscience mutated rapidly into something a lot more combative.

'Well, I am now I've made it through the front door security checks,' she agreed, simmering. 'Unlike my phone.'

Izzy looked bewildered. 'What's happened to your phone? Oh, Natasha, don't say you were mugged.'

Natasha looked straight at Kazim Whoever-he-was. 'Yup. A mugging. That's what it was.'

His eyes flickered. But he did not say anything.

Kind Izzy hugged her again, distressed. 'How horrible.'

Natasha did not take her eyes off Kazim. 'Nothing I can't handle,' she told him.

She meant it. She could see from that look in his eyes that he knew it too. His nostrils flared.

Clearly no one had said that they could handle Kazim before. He was outraged. Outraged enough to do anything about it? Natasha was not sure.

Then she saw the rigid look to his mouth. Oh, yes, definitely outraged enough to do something.

For a moment she felt a little frisson of alarm. But then she caught herself. She never ran from a challenge. Ever.

Fine, do your worst, she taunted him silently.

His nostrils flared.

A trickle of something that could have been alarm ran down Natasha's spine. Alarm or excitement. Suddenly all her senses were alert.

Nobody else seemed to notice. But she knew what was going on. And so did he. In the smoky darkness, unseen by anyone but themselves, light sabre clashed against light sabre.

It was like strong dark wine. Or a high wind.

Or coming alive.

CHAPTER THREE

ONLY not yet. Natasha had to get some warm clothes on before Kazim thought her trembling was down to him. He was arrogant enough for that.

Natasha turned her shoulder on him.

'Actually, Izzy, I could do with getting out of these clothes. Can you point me in the direction of my room?'

Izzy was instantly remorseful. 'Sure. You must be freezing.'

'I've been warmer,' agreed Natasha. 'In fact, I'd be glad to borrow a sweater too. I didn't know I'd need one.'

'And, of course, you kept your packing down to the minimum.' Izzy chuckled. She looked eloquently at Natasha's overnight case. 'How long have you been living out of that tiny little bag?'

Natasha grinned. It was a long-standing joke between them. 'A week.'

'Then a sweater isn't all you'll need to borrow,' said Izzy with feeling.

'The hotel had a laundry service,' retorted Natasha. 'A sweater will do it, really.'

'I'll come and find you some nice warm layers. And gum boots.'

Kazim interposed. 'Stay with your guests. I can show Ms Lambert to her room. There are plenty of spare sweaters in the Egyptian room.'

Izzy's brows flicked up, as if something in his tone surprised her.

Maybe it was the frosty disapproval, thought Natasha with irony. Presumably butlers weren't supposed to take an instant dislike to their employers' guests, even if the current employer was only borrowing their services for the weekend.

'The fireworks will start any moment,' Kazim said, as if that clinched it.

Natasha would much rather have had the girls' tête-à-tête with Izzy that she had promised herself. But she knew her social duty.

'Go and fix the fireworks,' she urged Izzy. 'If—Kazim, is it?—will just show me where to go…' she sent a bland smile in his general direction, carefully not meeting his eyes '…I'll get myself sorted in no time.'

'Okay,' said Izzy slowly. She looked thoughtful. 'Mulled wine out here afterwards, then. I'll bet you can do with it.'

Without waiting further, Kazim set off.

'Whoops. See you in a bit,' said Natasha and scampered after him, as fast as her stockinged feet permitted.

He led the way up the hill to a large paved terrace. Natasha followed. The damp grass struck cold underfoot. She regretted the impulse that had made her kick off her shoes. Temper always backfires, she thought ruefully. But it was too late now—and at least this time she was managing to keep up without slipping and sliding all over the place!

You're still a quick study, Natasha, she congratulated herself.

He was still striding ahead without speaking, though. She decided to open hostilities.

'So that was an adequate identification?' she said to his back.

He glanced over his shoulder at that. 'It was.'

'What a relief!'

He ignored the mockery. 'It must be.'

She realised suddenly that there was just a hint of a foreign accent to the deep voice, elusive as perfume. Maybe it was not even an accent. Just a slight over precision in pronunciation.

Natasha said abruptly, 'When did you decide to dislike me?'

He kept walking. 'If I am Lurch the butler, it is not my place to dislike you.'

It was neutral. Indifferent, even. So why was she suddenly positive that he was laughing at her? And why did a man with an arrogance quotient in the top one per cent decide to take a job as a butler?

Before she could ask, he held the door into the house open

for her to precede him. She glanced at him as she passed and was surprised at the sheer force of his physical presence. Yes, he was tall. Taller even than she had realised outside on the front steps. But it was not his height that had all her instincts on red alert.

Nor was it his looks. Though the light of the house revealed him to be one of the most extraordinarily good-looking men Natasha had ever met. Not the pretty, smooth-faced good looks of a fashionable heart-throb either. It was something harder, fiercer. The dark eyes might be cool. But there was a fire burning under that imperturbable façade, she thought.

I wouldn't like to cross him.

In spite of herself, Natasha shivered at the thought.

Instantly she was angry. It did not matter whom she crossed, said her internal mentor. She could handle herself. More important, she could handle the enemy! No matter what the world threw at her, she could handle it. Always had. Always would.

Relax, she told her instincts.

The door led to an old-fashioned orangery, all pale wood and glass. It was warm and full of sweet-leaved citrus trees. Overwhelmed for a moment, she paused in the doorway, all her senses alive to the scented air.

And Kazim walked into her.

It was like an assault, an electric shock straight to the naked nerves. She jumped, stumbled…cursed.

He caught her by the elbow and set her upright. 'Careful.'

His fingers were cold from the brutal night, but his hold was not. Natasha felt as if a fire inside him arced across and set light to something in her too. It literally took her breath away.

He looked at her, surprised. 'Are you all right?'

She gave that little shiver again. She did not answer. She could not.

Relax, damn you!

'You are jumpy, aren't you?'

Natasha found her voice—and brought herself gratefully back down to earth. 'Try bloody frozen,' she told him pleasantly.

He did not look as if he quite believed that. But he shrugged and led the way, threading between the orange and lemon trees as if they made up an obstacle course he could run blindfold. He opened the door into the main house with a flourish.

Still there was nothing Natasha could quite put her finger on. The gesture was just too theatrical. It was almost mocking.

She thought: It's as if I'm standing on a stage and performing to an audience of one.

What does he know that I don't?

But she was not going to let him see that he was getting to her. She went through the door he was holding and looked coolly round the oak-panelled entrance hall.

'Impressive!'

The walls were hung with Victorian hunting prints and massive portraits of sober citizens in civic regalia. She pursed her lips in a silent whistle. 'Whoever owns this place? They must be complete fossils.'

His spine was reinforced steel. 'The owner values tradition, certainly.' His tone said that she was a trashy modern thing, incapable of understanding.

Natasha decided it was time for a little mockery of her own.

'Fun bunch,' she observed, curling her lip at a severe family group. 'Even the gun dog looks as if he's wearing a corset.'

Kazim looked down his nose. 'Not an art lover, Ms Lambert?'

'Not a fan of pompous snobs,' she said crisply.

He glanced at the picture they were passing. 'The alderman does look as if he's on his best behaviour,' he admitted thoughtfully, to her surprise.

But before she could pursue her brief advantage, he led the way upstairs and turned along a discreetly lit corridor.

'Ms Dare thought you would enjoy the Egyptian room. She said you'd like the chandelier. And it has a real nineteen-twenties bathroom.'

Natasha was inclined to be scornful. 'What's special about a nineteen-twenties bathroom?'

Kazim's expression did not change. But Natasha knew she had made another mistake. Somehow, she had let him score a point.

'I will be happy to show you.' It was just too smooth, some-how. Like someone playing a butler on the stage.'

Her brows twitched together in quick suspicion. But before she could challenge him, he had opened a massive oak door. He flicked a light switch. It seemed to Natasha as if a dozen lamps came on at least. He stood back to let her precede him. She stood in the doorway, blinking in disbelief.

The room had *everything*. Not just a chandelier, a velvet-hung four-poster bed, some serious antique chests and a painting that looked like an original Monet.

She gulped. But she had no time for the room to overawe her. Her feet were hurting quite badly now. In fact her left heel was burning. She must have bruised it as she'd scrambled after him over the paths and the twig-strewn grass. Refusing to let him see what he had reduced her to, she strode into the room, con-centrating hard on not limping.

Kazim followed. He set down the small overnight case—with a great deal more ceremony than it deserved—on a bench at the end of the bed. He patted the rich brocade coverlet. As if he were testing the damned thing for bounceability, thought Natasha wrathfully. While he played the part of a classic butler in perfect tailoring.

'Thank you,' she said crisply, dismissing him.

He did not seem to notice. He just nodded, acknowledging her thanks. Was he laughing at her again?

Kazim opened a drawer, then several others, in quick succes-sion, as if he was unsure for once. Natasha barely noticed. Her nose twitched at the smell of lavender and mothballs.

'Traditional indeed,' she said, almost to herself. 'My grand-mother's house used to smell like that.'

Kazim did not like that. He shut the last drawer with consid-erable force.

'You will find spare sweaters in there. Shirts. Please help yourself.'

Natasha came back to the present with a little jump.

'Thank you,' she repeated with emphasis and opened the door wide, standing beside it pointedly.

He ignored the hint. Instead he crossed the huge room and flung open a pair of double doors she had not noticed before.

'And here is the answer to your question. Your bathroom!'

She could almost hear a flourish of trumpets, thought Natasha. It was clear that he was not going to move until she had inspected it.

She sighed ostentatiously. 'There's really no need to give me the guided tour. I know how taps work.'

'But these are exceptional taps.'

Did his lips twitch? She stared at him suspiciously. He stared back, the expressionless butler to the life. She mistrusted him deeply.

But she wasn't going to let him get the better of her.

A bathroom was too intimate, of course. But not more intimate than that proprietorial stroking of the bedspread. And she was quite sure that he knew it and was deliberately amusing himself.

Natasha pinned on a smile as deceptive as his own and limped over to stand beside Kazim. Not close beside Kazim. There was a crucial metre between their shoulders. She took good care of that.

'Thank you. Very nice. That—'

Then she took in the full wonder of the room before her. She stopped dead. Her jaw dropped.

'Decadent, would you say?' said her tormentor, pleased.

Natasha gulped. 'I've never—' She pulled herself together. She was not going to let the damn man make her lose her cool so easily. 'How interesting,' she said faintly. 'Egyptian?'

'Well, Hollywood Egyptian,' agreed Kazim. 'It was designed by a movie art director. Impressive, isn't it?'

Natasha shook her head, still staring. 'Everything but the sheikh,' she said with feeling, forgetting to be cool again.

For a moment he was no longer impassive. His lips twitched perceptibly. 'That could be arranged.'

Natasha came back to the real world with a jump. 'Sorry. What?'

He was striding round the bathroom, indicating its unique design with a helpful commentary. Natasha listened to one word in ten.

Every horizontal surface in the bathroom gleamed with marble—floor, ceiling, vanity table, even the window sill. The walls, where they weren't gleaming decorated mirrors, were covered with hieroglyphs and pictures of stylised Egyptian houris with more eye make-up than draperies. The sunken bath was circular; at the marble rim there were indentations that she realised suddenly were head rests. Two head rests, to be precise.

If she had been with Izzy, they would have sat down on the edge of that preposterous bath and laughed until they'd cried. But it was not a joke she could share with this not-quite-butler. Not Kazim, with his unreadable eyes and his private laughter. And his theatrical butlering.

The truth was he was just too damn sexy to be a butler. He challenged her. He made her uneasy. He made her *think*. And she needed to talk all of that through with some good friends over a bottle of wine.

Natasha was aware of a sharp pang of regret. Oh yes, she had really been looking forward to that girls' weekend. It would have been nice to take off her armour for once. She shifted unwarily and winced as her bruised heel complained.

She found he was looking at her oddly. Perceptively? That would never do. She didn't want this man to recognise that uncharacteristic moment of weakness.

She drew herself to her full height and said crisply, 'Thank you for showing me to my room. Now I would like to change.'

But he did not go. Indeed, he showed no sign that he even noticed he had been dismissed. 'Are you hurt?'

She was startled. 'What?'

'You flinched.'

'I didn't.'

He didn't contradict her. He just looked. Suddenly he was all male arrogance again.

Natasha responded to it, as she always did. Her eyes narrowed and her chin tilted dangerously. 'What?'

He ignored her, frowning. 'Now I think about it, you were limping in the orangery too.'

She glared. 'Okay, maybe I was. So what?'

'So how did you hurt yourself?'

'Well, now, there's a question. Could it be anything to do with being marched along an uneven path in the dark at light speed? Surely not!'

He frowned even harder. 'Are you saying it's my fault?'

Natasha gave a bark of laughter.

For a moment he looked furious. Then it was gone and he was the courteous butler again. 'Then I must do what I can to help you.'

'Why bother?' said Natasha, blunt as always.

'You are my guest.'

She bared her teeth at him in a smile that was ninety per cent challenge and ten per cent pure taunt. 'I'm Izzy Dare's guest.'

His eyes flickered. Annoyance, palpable as smoke, wafted off him.

Yes! Natasha chalked up a point to the female warrior. A small point, but worth having.

Content with her victory, she nodded to the door. 'Now, if you'll just go and help someone else, I'll be down in a few minutes.' The superior tone pleased her.

For the second time he failed to notice that she was dismissing him. Or not failed exactly. Ignored would be a better word.

Natasha drew herself to her full height. '*Thank* you—'

She got no further. He swung her neatly off her feet.

'Put me down,' said Natasha furiously, superior no longer.

He did. But not at all as she had intended.

He dropped her onto a stone seat with lion's paws for arms and went down on one knee before her.

He picked up one foot and stared blankly at her ruined tights. 'What on earth have you done?'

Natasha had not felt so grubby since she had scraped her knee in the playground and her mother had rebuked her. She glared. 'Lost my shoes, didn't I?'

She tried to take her foot back. She failed.

He inspected the foot narrowly.

'What do you think you're doing?' Natasha was trembling. With anger, she told herself. With anger.

Kazim rotated her ankle. He was quite gentle but very firm.

'No bones broken,' he decided.

Natasha was shaken. To disguise it—'Are you a doctor as well?' she said nastily.

He looked up then, a surprising glint of mischief in his eyes.

'No, but I've taken enough physical risks to know the basics.'

She took the opportunity to retrieve her foot. 'No bones broken,' she said curtly. 'You said it yourself. Now will you please…?'

He lifted her other foot.

She gasped and fell silent. There was not even a vestige of torn hose between their skins, this time. And his fingers were so warm she could feel the blood beating against her cold skin.

Natasha's mouth dried. She forgot what she was going to say; almost forgot how to think. All she could do was sit there, breathless, looking down at his bent head, and wonder at how crisp and dark his hair was, how surprisingly broad his shoulders. How sensitive his hands…

Natasha sat bolt upright. She was horrified. That was the sort of thing you thought about a lover. Or didn't, on the whole, at least in her recent experience. But not, never, a stranger.

I must be out of my mind.

'Stop that,' she rapped out.

He did not even look up. 'You're bleeding.'

'What?'

She bent down to peer at the foot. Their faces were suddenly close. She caught a hint of seriously expensive cologne.

Her brows twitched together. Since when did butlers wear Amertage?

Oblivious, Kazim said, 'Ah, there it is. You seem to have torn the skin. Hold still a moment.'

'What? Why? *Ouch!*'

She recoiled at the sharp pain.

He held up a savage-looking rose thorn and offered it to her. 'Big beast,' he said with satisfaction.

'Yes,' agreed Natasha faintly.

He was still concentrating on the task in hand. 'You need a bandage on this. I will have someone see to—' He stopped dead.

Suddenly Natasha was desperate to be alone.

'Don't bother. I've got a plaster in my case. I'll do it myself.'

He ignored that too, getting to his feet. 'Then I'll get it for you.'

Natasha flinched inwardly. She really, really didn't want this man going through her things. She travelled so light that almost everything in the bag was deeply personal. The contents revealed altogether too much about her, from the severe cotton underwear to rainbow silk scarves; to say nothing of those ludicrous furry feet.

But she couldn't say that, could she? It would just show him how exposed he made her feel—even invite him to probe further. So she watched helplessly as he went back into the bedroom and threw open the small case.

Trying to sound indifferent, she told the open bathroom door, 'There's a small first aid pack in there somewhere.'

He started emptying the case, putting her clothes in neat piles on the bed as he removed them.

'Very efficient, travelling with your own medical kit.'

'I am efficient.'

It made her stomach turn over, watching those long fingers among her silks and cashmere. And when he found the squashy pussy-cat slippers, he paused, staring as if he could not believe his eyes. He said nothing. But Natasha felt her face flame.

She looked round wildly for a distraction. She found it in Egyptiana.

'Who on earth put this lot together? Egyptian Bathroom Productions Inc? It's outrageous.'

He put the slippers down on the floor and chuckled.

It was a sexy sound. So sexy Natasha's hair lifted gently on the back of her neck.

Even as she fought down her own instinctive response, it

astonished her. Arrogance and sexiness did not go together in Natasha's book. Not normally. This man seemed to be turning all her normal reactions on their head. Again and again and again.

'It's pure art deco,' he said over his shoulder. 'I told you—specially commissioned from a Hollywood expert.'

Natasha swallowed. 'It would have to be. Either that or we have some serious grave-robbing here.'

'Ah, here it is.' He came back into the bathroom with her little first aid pouch.

She could still feel the remnants of that blush. It was all her own fault too! What sort of professional woman thought slippers with whiskers were absolutely indispensable gear for an international business trip?

What would he think of her? What did it matter what he thought?

But she hadn't admitted she owned a pair to anyone, not her mother, not even Izzy. Much less that she took them with her whenever she travelled. And now this mocking, unpredictable, *sexy* man was the only person in the world who knew her shameful secret. Well, that particular shameful secret. She winced.

'Thank you,' she muttered.

He looked at the wall frieze with appreciation. 'My—' He stopped abruptly. 'Er—the original owner was a reprobate, but he wasn't into grave-robbing.'

Natasha followed his gaze. The houris were slim as reeds and twisting themselves into graceful, muscle-killing knots. She eyed them sourly.

'Just young women wearing lots of eye make-up and not much else,' she supplied.

But they were beautiful, utterly confident in their languid hedonism. They were definitely not the sort of women to sit pounding at a computer at five o'clock in the morning in order to impress a client.

Natasha stroked a gentle finger down one lithe shape. She was suddenly rueful. 'Ever feel outclassed?'

Kazim's tone became positively comforting. 'They are not supposed to represent real women, you know.'

She jumped and came back to the moment.

'Thanks for the reassurance,' she said dryly.

'Unnecessary, I'm sure.'

God, you're smooth.

She didn't say it aloud. A polite visitor didn't make personal remarks to a butler—even a borrowed butler with a dodgy attitude and an expensive taste in toiletries.

She almost snatched the first aid pouch from him and quickly found a plaster. She ripped off the protective packaging and briskly inspected her heel.

Kazim watched in evident disapproval. 'Surely you're going to disinfect the wound before you put a plaster on?'

Natasha breathed hard. 'Look, it was a rose thorn, right? Not a poison dart.'

'Even so, it would be wise to wash it, at least. Your feet are very dirty.'

Once, when she was about eight, her mother had come to pick her up from school. It had been summer and her mother had been wearing a pretty voile dress smelling of apple blossom. Feverish with delight at the unexpected treat, Natasha had rushed off the athletics field and flung herself into her arms. Of course, she'd been sweaty and covered with sand from the long-jump pit. It hadn't been surprising that her mother had recoiled.

But it stayed, that tiny, involuntary, uncontrollable moment of revulsion. It stayed—and burned.

Natasha often wondered what would her mother have said if she had seen her only daughter in tee shirt and trousers that were no more than rags, unwashed for days, plodding through the jungle at the behest of an arrogant bullyboy. Because her life had depended on it. Recoil wouldn't have covered it. Oh, yes, slippers with whiskers on were only part of the things Natasha didn't tell her nearest and dearest.

And now here was Kazim, who had seen those furry feet, and wore the most expensive cologne in the world. Okay, his reaction was not quite full-blown recoil. But he did not like her dirty feet, that much was obvious. He was not trying too hard to hide his distaste.

'Thank you for pointing that out,' said Natasha wryly.

'I'll ring for someone—' He did another of those abrupt skids into silence.

But Natasha barely noticed. 'No need, thank you,' she said quietly. 'There are antiseptic wipes in the first aid kit. I can take it from here.'

He looked down at her foot. 'The wound is very awkwardly placed.'

Temper, uncontrollably sudden, bubbled up, startling her. 'I'm fine. I don't need anyone. I've put on my own sticking plasters all my life.'

'But—'

'And I'll shower. I'll scrub myself from head to toe, I promise. If you will just—go—*away*.' Her voice rose to a small scream.

Their eyes met like swords.

He did not go away. He did not move.

And then he astounded her. Utterly.

'When I first saw you,' he was reflective, 'I thought you looked like a robot.'

And in that gleaming, sparkling, voluptuous room, he touched one finger to the pulse that jumped at the base of her throat.

'You don't look like a robot now.'

Natasha heard herself give a gasp like a bursting balloon.

Kazim smiled and bent towards her. Slowly. Slowly. His eyes were guarded, but she sensed smouldering heat there. And there was a question in their depths, a question he demanded she answer...

Natasha leaned back and back until she thought her spine would snap. But she did not push him away. And she did not utter a word of protest.

For a moment they were utterly still; staring at each other; not speaking.

Kazim seemed to search her face. He looked serious; no longer teasing, questioning even. No hint now of the man whose lip had curled at her dirty feet. None of that spine-chilling arrogance. He looked as if he were setting out with her on an unknown path and wanted to know he could trust her…

Natasha caught her breath, shocked. She was moved by his expression, and that shocked her too.

Then, even as she watched his eyes flickered and he straightened. He was smiling again, but his eyes were masked. The smouldering fire was doused as if it had never been. The question, it seemed, had got its answer.

He gave her a pleasant smile. 'Surprising.'

He waited. But Natasha was all out of smart remarks. All out of anything except a vast astonishment.

'Don't you agree?' he prompted gently.

But all she could do was shake her head dumbly.

He looked oddly satisfied. And, before she could find her voice or think of a sensible thing to say, he had bowed his head and left.

Natasha found she had been holding her breath. She dragged in a long, grateful gust of air and bent over the marble unit, swallowing again and again.

Eventually her breathing came back under her control. What the hell happened? she thought, bewildered.

She took a long look at herself in the glimmering Venetian mirror. Her stylish hair was wind blown and had collected more than a few twigs. But they would brush out. Then the natural wheat-blonde hair would fall back into its usual elegant cap. That was why she paid a fortune to her hairstylist. It framed her face, emphasising the quirky cheekbones and diminishing the too-wide mouth, the too-decided nose, the lopsided, world-weary grey eyes.

'You have an *interesting* face, dear,' her mother used to say to her. 'Full of character.' And 'Prettiness is overrated,' said her pretty mother complacently.

Well, just at the moment, those world-weary eyes looked suspiciously uncertain. Natasha leaned forward, peering. Yes, no doubt at all. Kazim the butler had thoroughly unsettled her.

She was not having it. *Nobody* unsettled Natasha Lambert. What she needed to do now was shed the business suit. Look like a robot, indeed! She would turn herself into Natasha the Party Guest right now. And then wow the socks off every single man at the bonfire for once.

Including Kazim Whoever-he-was with his weird interest in people's passports and his nasty sense of humour. To say nothing of his flamboyant way of going about his butler's duties. And the smouldering fires she had glimpsed.

Involuntarily, Natasha looked back at the voluptuous bathroom. It was just built to fuel smouldering fires.

Whoops. Where did that come from?

Quite suddenly, she began to laugh.

'It's a long time since you've been on a charm offensive,' she told herself ruefully. 'Right. Time you got your eye in again.'

She soaked her filthy feet until they were pink and clean as a bathed baby. And she tried not to remember his hands on her. In fact, she whisked through her shower without ever once looking at herself in that mirror made for seduction. She set about unpacking with brisk efficiency

Then she found a sweater in the drawer. It was miles too big. The sleeves hung over her hands and she could pull its polo neck up to cover her entire face if she wanted. There was something reassuring about its smell—wool and soap powder and a hint of something else she couldn't quite catch but pleasingly familiar. It would do the job perfectly.

Underneath it she put on enough layers to keep warm. Found her fur-lined gloves. Went downstairs and tracked Izzy's offered wellington boots in the cloakroom off the main hall.

And went back to the party.

CHAPTER FOUR

DOMINIC TEMPLETON-BURKE was tending the barbecue. He looked up as Kazim approached.

'Where did you get to? The pyrotechnics people were looking for you. Want to know about placing the fireworks.'

Kazim shrugged. 'You decide. It's your party.'

'It's your house,' Dom pointed out dryly.

Kazim smiled. 'I am sure they are too professional to blow it up.'

'You're an optimist.'

'I'm a delegator,' Kazim corrected. 'I employ the best and then I trust them to do their job.'

'Plutocrat,' teased Dom.

'I don't deny it.' Kazim dismissed the subject. 'Tell me about Izzy's friend from New York.'

Dom was inspecting the coals, but at that he looked up, surprised. 'You mean Ms Hot Shot? You've met her?'

'I encountered her on the doorstep,' said Kazim carefully.

'Here? I thought she wasn't going to make it. Are you sure?'

'I hope so. Otherwise, I've just shown a potential assassin into the Egyptian suite,' Kazim said with irony.

Dom looked alarmed.

Kazim sighed. 'Relax. It was a joke. Izzy identified her anyway.'

Dom was intrigued. 'They're great mates. I haven't met her yet, though. What's she like?'

Kazim's mouth tilted. 'A blonde with attitude,' he said with relish.

'Izzy said she can be pretty feisty.'

'An understatement, believe me.'

'Ah.' Dom knew how to interpret that. They had been friends a long time. 'Locked horns with her already, have you?'

'Put it this way—she doesn't like me.'

Dom laughed aloud. 'Surprise me.'

Kazim was unoffended. 'Very amusing,' he said calmly. 'Now tell me everything you know about her.'

Dom was startled. He knew Kazim's taste in women. Natasha Lambert, from all he had heard about her, shouldn't have been a starter. He flipped steaks over, marshalling the facts as he knew them.

'Well, from what Izzy says she's a whiz market researcher. Owns her own company. Makes big bucks.'

Kazim recalled the quietly luxurious clothes in her overnight case—well, apart from the furry shoes with cat faces on them— the air of expecting to be obeyed. His lips twitched. 'That figures. There is no Mr Lambert?'

Dom shrugged. 'Your guess is as good as mine. Izzy seems to think she's a party girl *par excellence*.'

Kazim thought of the imperious blonde in the spotlight on the front steps. Power dressed and mad as a hornet! His lips twitched. 'She doesn't look like any party girl I've ever met.'

'And you've met plenty.'

'We both have.'

Their eyes met in perfect comprehension.

Dom was a gentleman. He said uncomfortably, 'Like I said, I don't know her but…word gets around. When she goes on the town there's usually a man in tow.'

'Ah.' Kazim digested that. '*A* man. Not necessarily the same one.'

'No,' said Dom, grateful to be so easily understood. 'Not often the same man twice, from what I hear.'

'Interesting.' Kazim sounded as if he meant it.

Dom was faintly alarmed. Kazim had the reputation of being a generous lover, quite apart from the roses and the poetry. But he didn't stay in one place for long and he was easily bored.

'Look,' he said. 'Natasha Lambert can buy her own diamond

bracelets if she wants them and she doesn't sound like she'd be impressed by poetry.'

Kazim raised haughty eyebrows. 'And your point is?'

'She's not your type. Don't get involved. It can only go wrong.'

Kazim stopped playing the sheikh and looked mischievous. 'So?'

'So then Izzy will get upset. And I'll have to take sides,' said Dom with feeling.

Kazim laughed. 'You've lost your taste for adventure.'

'Abrasive blondes were never my sort of adventure,' Dom said with justice.

'Then you've missed a lot,' said Kazim calmly. 'In the right circumstances, they can be rewarding.'

Dom groaned.

Kazim saw a small, determined figure marching down the slope on the other side of the bonfire. Her boots were too big and so was her borrowed outer gear. He knew that sweater. How had she managed to find one of his own among all the discarded jumpers in those drawers?

His smiled widened, grew wicked.

'Very rewarding,' he said with relish. 'Excuse me, I've got to go and see a woman about a poem.'

And left Dom open-mouthed.

Natasha strode briskly down towards the lake. In a borrowed Aran sweater she was as warm as toast. Besides, now that she knew where everyone was, the darkness didn't seem so threatening.

She had the forethought to take her little pencil torch with her, but it didn't show up much in the dense bushes. No sign of the designer shoes. 'Must remember to look for them tomorrow before I leave,' she told herself. 'To say nothing of my mobile phone. Probably all for the scrap heap but I might as well look. Butler? He's more like a demolition man.'

The thought came involuntarily: a very sexy demolition man. She blushed in the dark, winced and missed her footing on the muddy ground. The too-large boots sent her staggering. Her pencil torch raked the sky.

'Ah, there you are,' said Izzy cheerily, emerging from the darkness. 'Sending up distress signals, Tash?'

Natasha righted herself and breathed hard. This woman was her best friend, she reminded herself.

'Oh, good. You found a nice warm sweater, then,' said Izzy, oblivious.

'Eventually,' said Natasha grimly. 'After the tour of the bathroom and a lecture on medical hygiene. Tell me about the butler.'

Izzy's mouth fell open. 'What? Who?'

'The smooth character who showed me to my room.'

'*Kazim?*'

'That's the one.' A horrid thought occurred to Natasha. 'Are you saying he's not a butler?'

Izzy seemed quite unable to speak.

Natasha shut her eyes. The exquisite tailoring. Thousand-dollar cologne. That air of play-acting. *Of course,* he wasn't a butler. She had even known it, in her bones. If only she hadn't been so hung up on that damned arrogance, if only she hadn't been so determined to crush him, if only she had listened to her own instincts—she would have known.

She groaned aloud.

'He owns the place,' said Izzy faintly.

'Owns—' It was Natasha's turn to lose the power of speech.

'Oh, please say you haven't insulted him, Tash.'

Insulted him? I damn nearly kissed him.

Natasha pulled herself together and buried the thought deep.

'Why did he say he was the butler, then?'

'Did he?'

Natasha passed their exchanges under rapid review. 'Well, maybe not quite,' she admitted. 'But he knew that was what I thought.'

'I expect he was teasing. Dom says he has a great sense of humour.'

Pointing out the decadent splendours of that Egyptian fantasy and coming within a cat's whisker of kissing her? Oh, yes, a great sense of humour.

'I'm splitting my sides,' said Natasha grimly.

Izzy looked faintly apologetic. 'Dom says that Kazim has not been his usual self this weekend,' she said excusingly. 'He thinks he might be worried about something.'

'Yeah. He looks like a worrier.' Natasha was dry.

'Don't hate him, Tash,' Izzy begged, suddenly serious. 'He's Dom's best friend. And I really need your support, here.'

It was an appeal Natasha could not withstand. There had been a time in the jungle when all they had had to keep them going was their support for each other.

Natasha touched Izzy's arm briefly. 'Don't worry, Izzy. I'll be good.'

'Really?' Izzy peered at her in the darkness, half hopeful, half disbelieving.

Natasha squared her shoulders and said, with real heroism, 'Love him like a brother already.'

It was not long before her resolution was tested. She had eaten smoky sausages and asked Dom all the right things. She had lifted her glass to the two of them and drunk champagne so cold it made her throat close. She chatted and listened and laughed obligingly at other people's funny stories. But inside she was beginning to feel deathly tired and think longingly of that big inviting bed. She was trying to assess the chances of slipping back into the house without upsetting Izzy when—

'Looking for a guide?' said an amused voice in her ear.

Natasha stiffened. She did not turn to look at him. She had promised herself she would be nice and the temptation to spit in one of those laughing eyes might just get the better of her if she got too close.

'I take it that you are laughing at me,' she said to the distant bonfire. 'It's becoming a habit.'

He moved closer in the smoky dark.

'Ah. I deduce that Izzy has given you my résumé.' He sounded completely unrepentant.

'I didn't—and don't—want your résumé.' Her words dripped

disdain. 'I knew all I needed to once Izzy told me that you own this—place.' The last word was heavy with irony.

He chuckled. 'So okay. It's not modern enough for your taste. But you have to admit that the Egyptian bathroom, at least, was a unique experience.'

Natasha reminded herself that Izzy was her best friend and she wanted her to get on with Kazim—was *relying* on her to get on with him.

So she breathed hard and stayed civilised. Just. 'You never give up, do you?' she said at last.

'Give up?'

'Trying to embarrass me.'

He laughed softly. 'Believe me, I don't have to try. It seems to happen all on its own.'

'All right,' said Natasha in a goaded voice. 'I should never have called you Lurch the butler. That was no reason for you to take the ball and run with it. Don't you realise, that sort of wind-up could give a woman a serious hang-up?'

'It would take more than a little misunderstanding to give you a hang-up, I'm sure.'

'It was not a misunderstanding. It was deliberate deception.'

He threw back his head and roared with laughter. 'You're priceless!' he said, when he could speak.

Natasha stood four square in front of him. 'Do you deny that you deliberately made me think you were the butler?'

'I do. The butler thing was entirely your own idea.'

Natasha refused to back down. 'And you just let me go right on thinking it, didn't you? Did that give you a kick?'

Even in the dark she could see the wicked glint in his eyes. The flickering flames of the bonfire made him look like the devil incarnate. 'Best fun I've had this year.'

Natasha could not believe her ears. 'Best *fun*…?'

'I don't get out much,' he said excusingly.

She did not believe him for a moment. If ever there was a party animal, it was this man, who slipped effortlessly into playing the butler because he thought it was *fun*.

She could have danced with frustration—if she hadn't thought she might dance right out of the borrowed boots.

She found he was watching her with deep appreciation. 'Go ahead,' he urged. 'Scream. You know you want to.'

It was pure provocation. After a moment's suffocating outrage, Natasha even realised it.

'No, thank you.' Her tone was impeccably polite.

'Sure?'

Oh, he was a games player, all right. She had better leave him before she did something she would regret in the morning. Like slapping him hard across his handsome, laughing mouth.

She turned away. The too-large boots squelched and she lurched a little.

At once he was at her shoulder, his arm strong and steadying. His body was warm. How did he stay so warm in only a suit, when all the others were bundled up against the cold? How did that warmth blaze through her, as if his blood had suddenly made a connection to her blood? Her ears rang. She stared at him, in horrified realisation.

'Careful,' he said.

The pull of attraction was so strong it nearly knocked her off her feet. Careful, indeed!

But, however shaken she was, she had years of practised self-control behind her.

'Relax,' she said after only the slightest pause. She removed his arm. 'I'm skidding inside these damn boots. Not about to collapse in a heap all over the lawn. You've got no excuse to jump on me this time.'

'What makes you think I need an excuse?' he purred.

Natasha was getting her second wind. 'Oh, pu-lease. Not that old line.'

'You're a hard woman.' He sounded wounded.

Natasha shone the beam of her torch on his face. He was trying to keep his face straight. Well, not trying very hard, actually. His eyes gave him away. He was laughing like mad.

Natasha saw red. She drew herself to her full height, disposed her weight carefully in those treacherous boots and stepped forward.

And said with great calm, 'Hard enough to handle you, sunshine.'

He blinked. It was obvious that people did not normally talk to Kazim Whoever-he-was like that.

Natasha saw it with satisfaction. She smiled. 'Mess with me at your peril.'

She switched off the light and turned her back, stamping off up the hill at slightly rocky speed.

He caught up almost at once. 'What sort of peril?' he said, interested.

Natasha ignored him. She speeded up as best she could, given her uncooperative footwear.

He kept pace with her easily. 'I mean, ballpark risk here.'

Natasha breathed hard and put her head down to climb the hill to the house.

She did not shake off Kazim. 'Are we talking a knee to the balls?' he asked. 'Loss of face? Bad publicity? Broken heart?'

'All of the above,' said Natasha, goaded.

'Sounds exciting,' said her tormentor, as if he were congratulating her. 'Where do I sign up?'

Natasha breathed hard. 'Oh, go away,' she said, exasperated.

But he laughed and stuck with her as she steamed on, away from the bonfire and the party, wishing she could get away from him as easily.

'Where are you going?' He sounded interested. 'I'm all for being alone, but do you think this is quite the weather for a tryst in the shrubbery?'

Natasha did not waste time telling him polite lies about lost handbags. 'I'm going to bed,' she said baldly.

He chuckled. 'Nice idea, but not yet, I think.'

'Not yet—?' It took her a critical ten seconds to pick up his meaning. By the time she did he was laughing openly.

Natasha's eyes narrowed to slits. 'Am I supposed to feel flattered? Or shocked to the core?'

'I'm sure you're much too sophisticated for either,' he said, odiously charming. 'Maybe a little intrigued?'

Her breath was unexpectedly difficult for a moment. 'No,' she said at last. 'I'm not intrigued at all.'

'Then I can see I shall have to try harder.'

For a moment Natasha was sorely tempted to call his bluff. Kazim, she was beginning to realise, was a control freak with a nasty sense of humour. But he could not be serious about making love to a woman he had only just met and didn't much care for, except to laugh at her expense. If she turned and said, 'Okay, come on, then, take me to bed,' he would have to back off.

Only she wasn't a hundred per cent sure that he would back off. Ninety-five per cent sure, maybe. But not a hundred. And Natasha was not going to bet on anything less than a cast-iron certainty here.

So instead she said crisply, 'I've had a hard week and I'm wiped. I need to sleep.'

'No, you don't.'

'What?' She stopped abruptly. The boots skidded to a halt a split second after she did. Natasha rocked.

He seized the opportunity to put an arm round her. It was—almost—avuncular. Natasha knocked it away.

'What do you mean, no, I don't?' she said with heat. 'How do you know how I'm feeling? I have every right to have jet lag.'

'Oh, you have a right, sure. Only you haven't got jet lag. You're in a temper and you want to rush off and sulk on your own,' he said, in a beastly kind voice, as if he really were her uncle.

'I have got jet lag—' Even to Natasha's ears it sounded childish.

'People with jet lag don't charge up forty-five-degree slopes as if their life depended on it.'

It was unanswerable. She decided she hated him.

'Are you jealous of Isabel?' he asked mildly.

She gasped. 'You're crazy,' she choked.

'Then you hate Dom.'

'I don't know Dom.'

In the darkness she saw the glint of white teeth. The blasted man was *smiling*.

'Then stay and see their fireworks.' The tone was almost caressing.

Yes, absolutely no doubt about it. She hated him more than any man she had ever met. And boy had he got some competition. He beat every single macho bully of them hands down.

As she glared at him in the darkness he said idly, 'Did you know that Isabel made Dom wait to announce their engagement because she wanted you to be here? The fireworks were supposed to happen last night.'

Natasha stopped seething for a moment, in sheer astonishment. 'What?'

'This—' he gestured to the party at the distant bonfire and then to a cordoned-off area, which she had not noticed before '—was all set to go last night. Until you failed to arrive. Or send a message.'

Natasha was utterly silenced.

'The fireworks were delayed for you. Only for you.' He wasn't idle any more. He wasn't laughing either. 'Can you really walk out on that?'

Even shaking with justified rage, Natasha had to admit it was a good point. A killer of a point.

'Damn you,' she said wearily. 'You win.'

'Excuse me?'

But she wasn't saying it again. 'Do you always get people to do exactly what you want them to?'

'I try.'

'Well, congratulations. You're good.'

He gave a ghost of a laugh. 'I'd better be.'

She didn't understand that and wasn't going to indulge him by asking. She pushed a hand through her hair. She was so tired she could feel the flesh dragging at her bones.

But Izzy was her friend. And no matter how mocking and self-serving men might be, your friends stuck by you. If Izzy

wanted Natasha by her side when the rockets went up, then Izzy
should have her.

But she didn't have to be by Kazim's side too. She left him
and found her friend.

'Great party,' she said brightly. 'Tell me what I can do to
help tomorrow. I see everyone had a job tonight.'

'Self-help,' agreed Izzy brightly, after only the slightest hesitation. 'Poor Kazim doesn't know what's hit him. The boys are
clearing up tonight and Pepper did lunch yesterday. So maybe
you could do breakfast? I know you get up with the dawn.'

'A long way before dawn in November,' said Natasha dryly,
glad to be given a practical problem. 'Okay, you're on. Full
English Gentlemen's Breakfast for—how many?'

'Oh, five or six maybe. Depends who gets up.

'A dozen once they smell the bacon,' said Natasha, a realist.
'Full English for twelve tomorrow. Leave it with me.'

There was no time for more. A rocket shot into the sky and
bloomed into a dandelion head of gold and silver and green.
There was a collective 'ah!' and everyone took their places to
watch. More rockets sprayed the sky with moon dust. Catherine
wheels whirled and glittered like Cinderella dancing at her ball.
Roman candles fizzed. The air was full of laughter and the smell
of cordite.

Izzy stood in front of her Dom, dropping her head back
against his shoulder. Watching, Natasha saw him fold his arms
round her and they stood, embraced, looking at the flowering
sky. Still looking at the fireworks, he dropped a light kiss on
Izzy's hair. She did not turn to look at him, just tipped back a
little further, like an animal buffing its head against its mate's
fur. It was utterly trusting.

Natasha felt cold to her bones. 'Don't,' she wanted to cry.
'Don't make yourself vulnerable.'

But, of course, she didn't. She turned her head away.

And found herself looking into dark eyes that were no longer
laughing.

'You again,' she said without pleasure.

Kazim was thoughtful. 'Are you absolutely sure you're not jealous of Isabel?'

Natasha gave a hollow laugh. 'I'm sure.'

Her eyes smarted. She rubbed them with fingers that shook slightly.

He stepped closer. 'You're crying.' He sounded surprised. Worse, he sounded intrigued.

'Smoke,' said Natasha crisply. 'Makes my eyes water. Kills my throat too.' She gave a small angry cough to illustrate her point.

He looked sceptical. 'You think she will be unhappy.' It was not a question.

Natasha shook her head. She looked over her shoulder uneasily, but Izzy was deep in conversation.

'Is it Dominic you dislike? Or any man who takes your friend away from you?'

'Stop it,' she said, beginning to be alarmed. 'Neither.'

'I don't believe you.'

'I don't dislike Dom,' she said in a goaded under voice. Izzy could be back at any moment.

'Then it is any man.' He nodded, as if that was exactly what he had expected.

'I am concerned for her, that's all,' said Natasha carefully. 'Marriage is a high-risk activity.'

In the shadows she saw his eyes narrow. 'Marriage? Or men?' There was just the faintest hint of scorn in his voice.

She should have left it there. She nearly did. But that hint of scorn was too much from a man who had spent half the evening pretending to be his own butler.

She rounded on him.

'You want the truth? Okay, here's the truth. In my experience, men are only useful for three things. And a woman can do them all herself without having to hand over a licence to blast her life to bits.'

His head reared back as if she had shocked him.

Good, thought Natasha.

She was sorry about her promise to Izzy. But some promises

were just doomed. This was not a man she could ever love like a brother.

'Blast her life to bits?' He sounded stupefied.

'Yes.' She was curt. 'So totally not worth it.'

'Which three things?'

'What?'

'You said there were three things men were useful for,' he reminded her.

Natasha glared. 'Emptying mouse traps. Opening champagne bottles. A quick sexual thrill.'

His eyes danced. 'And—?'

'And I can rent a feline mouser; I turn the bottle not the cork, and John Donne lasts longer.'

'Donne?' He looked interested. 'You like poetry?'

'Does it for me every time.'

He raised his eyebrows. 'I'm glad to hear it. But even so, are you sure that there is really no room for a man in your life?'

Natasha said sturdily, 'He'd be completely surplus to requirements. No question.'

He looked down at her, thoughtfully, almost pityingly. For a moment she almost thought he was going to pat her on the head. Her eyes dared him to try.

But he did something even more unsettling. He touched her lower lip with a caress like a moth's wing. Natasha flinched as if she had scalded herself. The little touch was somehow more intimate than a kiss.

He gave a soft laugh, that nobody but the two of them could have heard.

'It would take me one night to change your mind,' he murmured, his breath stirring the hair that curled round her ear. 'Just—one—night.'

Natasha gasped. She sought vainly for a crushing retort.

But it was too late. He was gone.

CHAPTER FIVE

KAZIM'S mind was not really on his messages as he skimmed through them that night. The power blonde was certainly a challenge. If the reconciliation talks weren't filling his diary for the next six months, he would be mounting a serious siege. Not his type, of course. But it was a long time since a woman had made him laugh so much, or stirred his blood. For a moment this evening he had felt heady, even reckless, like an anonymous student again, instead of a public figure with international responsibilities.

And there was that chink in her armour—she liked poetry.

'Definitely a challenge,' murmured Kazim, pressing the reply button to Tom's latest text.

Tom answered at once. 'What?'

Kazim brought himself back to reality. 'Nothing. Got your message. Trouble?'

'Not yet. But Suleyman has gone off the radar. Our sources say it's nothing, but I have a feeling he's planning something big. Let me know the moment anything unusual happens, right?'

'Don't I always?' said Kazim. Goodbye student recklessness. Hello responsible citizen. 'See you tomorrow, Tom.'

He cut the call and went to his room. It was only one door down from Natasha's. In fact, there was a connecting door to the Egyptian bathroom. Just for a moment, he wondered what she would do if he unlocked that door and stepped through. He was intrigued to find that he could not guess.

That in itself was almost enough to persuade him. That and the thought of those uneven grey eyes widening, as they did when she forgot to guard her expression. And that mouth…

He banged his fist on the window. 'Damn all diaries. Rats to responsibility. Grrr.'

Well, he was not going to sleep. And it was a long time since he had started a new poem. He sat down at the Chippendale desk, pulled a piece of paper towards him and began to play with phrases.

Natasha slept badly. The bed was too soft and when she woke, as she did too often, it seemed to her that the pillows smelled of Amertage. When she finally gave up trying to sleep, there was still a faint moon in the sky.

She got up. It was a relief. The house was silent and no one would want breakfast for ages. But at least she could get to know the unfamiliar kitchen and check on the stores.

The kitchen looked eerie in the grey pre-dawn light. But Natasha refused to be intimidated. She switched on the light and prowled round, taking stock. It was a big kitchen with a huge pine table in the middle and every culinary machine she could think of. It also had several walk-in pantries and three substantial chest freezers.

'Serious dinner-party country,' diagnosed Natasha. 'Kazim al Saraq lives in style.'

The early-morning radio was playing Gershwin. Natasha began to enjoy herself, doing a soft shoe shuffle as she tracked down the ingredients for breakfast. She collected bacon and butter, eggs and sausages, cereal and milk; then piled them all on a semicircular table against the wall.

She tracked down mushrooms and tomatoes and skimmed round the pine table like a glider coming in to land, whistling. Still dancing, she juggled sliced loaves, ending with a fancy manoeuvre that sent one high above her head. Tongue between her teeth with concentration, she danced forward and caught the loaf behind her back.

'Yes!' said Natasha, pleased with herself.

There was a burst of applause from the doorway. 'Very polished.'

Natasha spun round in shock; staggered; lost her footing.

Strange kitchens were dangerous. Fold-away furniture was worse. Her convenient table by the wall wasn't so convenient after all, it turned out. There was no notice on the thing saying, 'This table is hinged. If you bump into it, it will collapse.'

And Natasha bumped into it all right. Cannoned into it at full tilt. Kazim al Saraq applauded her private cabaret and it sent her into a flat spin. Literally. Her hip connected with the table and there was a sharp crack.

'Aaaargh,' said Natasha.

In the wink of an eye, the kitchen floor was covered. Bread burst out of its packaging. Cornflakes scattered. Two dozen eggs smashed and turned the goo to mosaic.

'Oh, no!'

Natasha's hands flew to her cheeks as she surveyed the wreckage.

'I see you like to go for the big finish,' said Kazim dispassionately. 'Impressive.' He strolled into the kitchen and raised his eyebrows at the unsavoury debris. His face was absolutely without expression. But she knew he was laughing. Again.

That was when Natasha began to realise the full extent of the disaster. Apart from shorts and workmanlike socks and running shoes, he was naked.

Naked and steaming slightly. His chest was an even gold. And it gleamed. In spite of herself, Natasha could not tear her eyes away. He had never looked less like a butler.

Wow, said her treacherous heart.

The house must have a gym somewhere, she thought distractedly, scrabbling for something prosaic to calm her overheated senses. Either that or he had been out running in the cold November morning. And what sort of man went running in the dark?

A man who did exactly what he wanted to at all times, that was who, she thought mordantly.

She could not think of a single thing to say. She cleared her throat noisily.

'I—um—I didn't know anyone else was up.'

Kazim was buffing his damp face with a towel. He was not ostentatiously muscled but, stripped like this, there was a compact power to him. Natasha's mouth dried.

He was surveying the ruined floor with open amusement now. The amusement of a man who had never had to clean up after himself.

'You don't do things by halves, do you?'

'I didn't do it deliberately. You startled me.'

'Not for the first time.'

He lobbed the towel away from him. It fell neatly onto a swing bin and was swallowed at once.

Natasha decided it was time to fight back. 'You're throwing that away?' she said in a shocked tone. 'Just because you've used it once?'

He was puzzled. 'What?'

'Have you no conscience about the planet?' said Natasha, stoking the fires of indignation gratefully. 'Wealth is no excuse for wasting the earth's resources, you know.'

His eyes danced. 'Not guilty. That's the laundry dump for my exercise clothes.'

Which, of course, left her feeling a complete fool.

'Oh.'

He skirted the noxious mess on the floor and strolled over to her. 'You really do like to hand out the criticism, don't you? Are you always this judgemental?'

He was close enough to touch if she wanted to. Natasha put her hands behind her back in pure instinct.

Kazim, she saw, was totally at ease. Well, he would be, it was his house. He had a perfect right to wander around in it with as few clothes on as he liked.

And she was a twenty-first-century woman. A man without his shirt wasn't going to send her into paroxysms of maidenly embarrassment, Natasha told herself with resolution.

Only Natasha felt her face flood with heat. Irritation, she assured herself. Nothing to do with the surprisingly powerful body. Okay, he was too close and much too revealed for her peace of mind. But he did not need to know that.

What worried her was, *why?*

He did not move a step closer; nothing she could object to. But his eyes grew intent...alert... Suddenly she felt as if she were on a precipice, without the slightest idea how she had got there.

It was all too much, somehow. The house was too silent. He was too vital. She was much too aware of both. And, even at arm's length, she was much too close to all that warm golden danger.

The kitchen was big, but not big enough. Not the way he was looking at her.

It was the last straw!

'Some days,' she said with concentrated fury, 'a sensible woman just shouldn't get out of bed.'

One eyebrow quirked. 'In other circumstances I would say that was a very neat invitation.'

This time Natasha realised that it was a deliberate wind-up before she went into full shock horror mode. Her eyes flashed, but at once she had her anger under control. She was good at control, she reminded herself.

'That line went out with the silent movies.'

For a moment he watched her mouth as if it fascinated him. Another good trick, thought Natasha, and watched his right back.

The gentle mockery died abruptly. He pulled a tee shirt down over the muscular torso and his eyes flared.

'And you can stop smouldering at me,' she added, goaded.

Something happened in his face. He took three steps forward. Suddenly she was back against the wall with nowhere to go and her eyes fixed on that firm, sensual mouth.

She didn't see it coming.

Why didn't she see it coming? Did she really think that smart remarks would keep him at arm's length? When she knew that the little flare of lust hadn't left his eyes? She could see it. No matter how much he'd enjoyed their fencing bout, he'd never lost focus. Not really.

Natasha removed herself from his embrace and gave herself a little shake.

'Thank you,' she said composedly. She stepped away from him and gave him a bland smile. 'More of the old-fashioned seduction technique, I see. More than a touch of the silent movies, if you want me to be honest,' she said kindly.

His eyes narrowed.

She saw a broom propped in the corner and prudently armed herself with it. No harm in being prepared.

'I'm sure it's very understandable.' She sounded sweetly reasonable, but she still watched him warily.

He was thunderstruck. 'Understandable?'

She gave him her brightest smile. 'Tall, dark and handsome. And wealthy with it. No woman ever says no to you, does she?'

There was a moment of total, devastating silence. His eyes did not blink.

Natasha thought, I wish I hadn't said that. He's not going to forget it—or forgive. I could just have made myself a bad, bad enemy.

She decided there were more important things to do than obsess about what Kazim al Saraq thought of her. She lifted her foot from the sticky, squelchy floor and made a face.

'I'd better get this cleared up.'

His face was utterly without expression. 'And find some replacement breakfast,' he interpolated.

There was the tiniest fraction-of-a-second pause.

'Thank you for reminding me,' said Natasha with awful politeness.

He did not offer to help. Presumably, scrubbing floors was women's work, thought Natasha with irony.

'I will go and shower,' he announced.

He neatly avoided stepping in the mess. It brought them too close again. Natasha's nostrils caught a fugitive flicker of a grassy fresh-air cologne before it was overtaken by the overpowering smell of male animal.

Their eyes met. Awareness jolted through her. Through him too, she was almost sure. Just for a second the veneer of sophistication was stripped away and they were primitive creatures, circling each other in the battle of desire.

Then she swallowed hard and stepped away.

'Go shower,' she said in a hard voice. 'I've got work to do.'

And, to her amazement, he did.

CHAPTER SIX

NATASHA cleared up the mess on the floor. It was a long time since she had done any housework and her method was rubbish. But she made up for it with the energy of simple fury.

How dared he? Oh, how *dared* he?

She did not ask herself what exactly it was that Kazim al Saraq had dared. Subconsciously she knew, of course. He had stirred her up; made her uncertain; made her *feel*. And she was not going there, ever again.

Instead she sat down and took stock of the practical problems. She had twelve people expecting a lavish breakfast and minimal supplies. She also had neither car nor phone and no knowledge at all of the area.

'This,' said Natasha ruefully, 'is a major initiative test.'

Then she thought of the pub the limo had passed yesterday on the way here. Surely it was more or less at the bottom of the drive? And country pubs knew everything. Even if they couldn't sell her what she needed they could tell her where there was a shop and even book a cab for her, if necessary.

Of course, she thought, she could prowl through the house until she found a phone and the local telephone directories. That would be a lot easier. But it was Kazim al Saraq's house and she risked bumping into him again. Even worse, she risked having to ask him for help in solving her problems.

'No way,' said Natasha with decision and piled into layers of clothes against the November winds.

In the end, it was quite simple. Apart from the electronic gates at the end of the drive—she kicked at one while hauling at the other; then propped them apart for her return with a substantial log—her plan worked like a dream. The pub landlord was intrigued to meet a visitor from Serenata Place. The village knew that the house was owned by a foreign gentleman, but he was seldom in residence and the staff were very cagey about him. There was clearly a deal to be struck here.

Natasha swapped a judicious amount of gossip on Kazim al Saraq and the firework party for milk, eggs, bread, sausages and various other tasty treats. There was even a ride back thrown in.

The kindly landlord drove her to the gates and, when he saw how she had propped them open to squeeze through, helped her haul them the rest of the way to admit his car. Then he drove her all the way to the kitchen door. He even helped her unload her purchases.

The kitchen was empty. Everything was exactly as she had left it. So the household was still in bed, Natasha thought, on a small sigh of relief.

She turned to her rescuer. 'Thank you,' she said with real gratitude. 'You're a real knight errant. Do you have time for a cup of coffee?'

He hesitated, clearly torn between his Sunday schedule and curiosity about the house. 'Maybe just a quick one.'

But Natasha had barely had time to put on the coffee maker before they were no longer alone.

'Good morning,' said Kazim al Saraq, breezing into the kitchen, in discreetly expensive casual gear, his smile wide and his eyes watchful. 'Found a friend?'

'Well, we've only just met. But he saved me a three-mile walk to the nearest farm shop, I'm told.' Natasha sent her rescuer a friendly smile.

The landlord didn't smile back. Indeed, he hardly glanced at her. Instead he was scrambling to his feet, not taking his eyes off Kazim. Natasha didn't blame him, for all the smiling, Kazim exuded hostility. Menace, even.

'Don't bother about the coffee,' said her rescuer hastily. 'I think I'd better be going, after all.'

'Oh, but—'

Kazim overrode her. 'We mustn't keep you from your own affairs any longer,' he agreed affably. 'My guest is very grateful.'

That's me, thought Natasha, annoyed. *My guest!* As if I'm too silly and female to speak for myself.

She was still fulminating inwardly as the man left. The moment she heard the car drive away, she turned on Kazim.

'Oh, for heaven's sake. He is the landlord of the pub down the road. All he did was to give me a helping hand. Most people would have said thank you. Why did you have to snarl at him?'

The smile disappeared as if it had never been. 'Reasonable precautions,' he said, almost absently.

Natasha snorted. 'You're paranoid.'

His head reared up at that, like a horse hearing the huntsman's horn. Suddenly his eyes were dangerous. 'And you're headstrong,' he said very, very quietly.

There was something here she did not understand. But Natasha refused to let him intimidate her. She began unpacking the food with quick, angry movements.

'Oh, pu-lease. What century are you in?'

'You know nothing about him.' The words bit.

Natasha set out pans and ingredients with savage precision.

'Well, I've only just met him. What do you want me to do? Ask him for his CV and a set of references?' She snapped her fingers in mock recollection. 'Oh, yes, I should have asked him for his passport.'

'That would be preferable to picking up any stranger who happens to offer you a ride,' said Kazim with deadly quietness. 'Or is that what you normally do?'

He's calling me a tart. Natasha was so angry she could barely speak.

'Get out of this kitchen *now*. Or I will. And then there won't be any breakfast for anyone.'

He snorted. 'Childish too.'

But he went. He went as if he could not get away fast enough.

Natasha cooked the most sumptuous breakfast of her life. She never afterwards remembered how and the odds against her repeating it were astronomical. But sheer temper fuelled a culinary performance that startled Izzy and Jemima and earned her high praise from everyone else.

Natasha accepted with gratitude. She knew how big a part luck had played in her production of edible food.

Afterwards, she escaped to the damp garden to look for her lost belongings. She found her designer shoes, soaked and caked with mud and dead leaves. She sighed over them ruefully. There might be a way of reviving them, but she doubted it. Of her cell phone, however, there was no sign.

This was a more serious problem. The number of her limousine service was stored in the cell phone. Natasha had not bothered to memorise it; any more than she had bothered to memorise the new name of the car company when it had restructured last year. So she could not even call directory enquiries.

'I feel an idiot,' she told Izzy, who was wandering around with a mug of coffee and a dazed expression of delight.

Behind them, Kazim gave his Sunday paper an enthusiastic rustle as if he were endorsing Natasha's assessment of herself.

Everyone had converged on the study after breakfast. It was a large room and Dom had built a professional log fire in the huge fireplace. Now they were all grouped round it, with various books or bits of the paper. The fire sputtered merrily and the smell of pine filled the room.

It would have been heavenly, if only Kazim al Saraq had not been sitting there like a giant spider, waiting for her to make another mistake, thought Natasha. But he was, and she could not wait to get away from Serenata Place.

Failing her own car company, she tried the locals. They were all booked. She phoned directory enquiries and got some numbers for London taxi companies. None of them could guarantee a car until late that evening.

'London?' said Kazim, putting down his paper. He was all charm and unreadable eyes. 'I will be happy to drive you myself.'

Izzy was patently relieved. Natasha could have screamed. But she had just proved there was no other way out of the place. And she was a grown-up, whatever he thought of her. She could manage a two-hour car trip in his company without losing her cool again, surely?

'Thank you,' she said, without expression.

He insisted that they wait until everyone else had gone.

'There's no need, honestly,' said Izzy. 'Dom and I can clear up and wait for the staff to come back.'

But, 'I am your host,' said Kazim. And that was the end of the matter.

So they waved the others off as they left, in dribs and drabs. Izzy and Dom were the last to go, in a battered off-roader piled to the roof with Dom's survival and mountaineering gear.

It felt odd standing on the doorstep beside Kazim; almost as if they were a couple. Natasha gave a superstitious shiver and moved away from him. He did not appear to notice.

He glanced at his watch. 'The staff will be back in ten minutes. I need to debrief them. Then we can go.'

Natasha nodded. The sky was darkening and a cold breeze whipped the dry leaves into little whirlwinds before letting them fall. She clasped her arms round herself. The November garden was forbidding. She felt very alone.

'You're cold,' he said. 'Let's go inside.'

He held the front door open for her to precede him.

'Thank you.' She shivered again, though the house was warm as toast.

'I just need to check a few things,' he said. 'Are you packed?'

'Over there,' said Natasha, nodding at her overnight case, where she had left it under the big hall table. 'I've been packed since breakfast.'

He frowned. 'You have not enjoyed your stay.'

Oh boy, understatement of the century.

'It has been very interesting,' she said carefully, 'but I always pack first thing in the morning. It's a habit I've got into because I travel so much for my work.'

'You console me,' said Kazim dryly, not sounding as if he cared a jot. 'Go and sit by the fire. I'll be with you in twenty minutes. See you here.'

Natasha nodded. But he was already gone.

Kazim was not surprised to see Tom Soltano with the returning staff. He had fully expected the Head of Security to supervise sweeping the house for unwanted electronic devices the moment the weekend guests had gone. He had not expected, however, to share his concerns.

But then Tom said, 'The electronic gates were opened at eight twenty-three and stayed open for more than an hour. We're trying to find out how they did it.'

Kazim was not surprised, but he was worried. 'I'm afraid I've got bad news too. I think there may have been a breach of the house, Tom.'

Soltano stayed calm. 'What happened? Window left open? Lock forced?'

Kazim shook his head. 'Simpler than that. One of the guests went for a walk this morning and the landlord of The Feathers brought her back.'

Tom's eyes were suddenly alert. 'How much of the house did he get into?'

'Only the kitchen as far as I could tell. But—'

'We'll go through it with eyebrow tweezers,' Tom promised cheerfully. Electronic security was his hobby as well as his job and he enjoyed the prospect of a challenge. He got out his Palm Pilot and started to make notes. 'Who was the guest?'

'Natasha Lambert,' said Kazim. He was surprised how reluctant he was to name her to his Head of Security. 'Long-standing friend of Isabel Dare. Runs a market research business. Successful. Very elegant.' And combative. And impetuous. And vulnerable. And very sure she was none of those things.

But Tom was security-trained. He knew when something was held back.

'Okay,' he said encouragingly. 'Friend of the bride, for sure.

Businesswoman of the year, maybe. Who does she hang with? What are her politics?'

Kazim shook his head.

'Travels, does she?'

There was no point in trying to deny it. Kazim shrugged. 'A lot, she tells me.'

Tom did not look up from his hand-held screen. 'And she got here when?'

'Saturday evening,' said Kazim with even more reluctance. 'She was a day late. Some sort of overrun with a client in New York, I believe.'

'Do we happen to know which client?' Tom asked casually.

'No. But no doubt you will by Monday lunch time,' said Kazim, suddenly irritated.

Tom grinned at him. 'Oh, I'll know sooner than that.'

He sympathised with Kazim's impatience with security procedures. They must be an intolerable intrusion on the private life of a young, virile man, thought Tom, glad his own life was less public. But it was still his job to protect Kazim and he would do it to the best of his ability.

'What else do we know about her?'

Kazim smiled reluctantly. 'Well, she's blonde.'

Tom stared. 'You're joking.'

'No. I said that if they sent a fashionista to assassinate me she had better be blonde—and then, lo, this woman appears.' He chuckled suddenly. 'Could someone have bugged the Land Rover?'

'I'll have it checked,' said Tom, not chuckling at all. 'And where is Ms Lambert resident?'

'London mainly, I think.'

'Address?'

'No, but I'm driving her back.'

Tom sucked his teeth. 'Not sure that's a good idea. There could be an ambush. If she's wired for global positioning, they will know exactly where to find you.'

'I really don't think that's likely,' said Kazim. 'You should have seen the lengths she went to to get out of travelling back with me.'

Tom digested this, clearly brooding on possible scenarios.

'I really don't see her as a secret agent,' said Kazim, thinking of those slippers with pussy-cat faces. Surely a hard-edged activist wouldn't wear fur feet with whiskers? 'She's not the type.'

Tom tapped the electronic pen against his teeth. 'What type is she, then?'

'Very much her own person. Doesn't take orders well, I'd say. Short fuse. Independent.'

A sudden thought, new and unwelcome, appeared to present itself to Tom.

'Do you find her attractive, Kazim?' he said bluntly.

Kazim hesitated. It was for barely two seconds, but those two seconds said everything. So he shrugged.

'Yes. Extremely.'

Tom looked appalled.

Kazim was amused and irritated in equal measure. 'Sorry about that,' he said dryly.

Tom rallied. He was a practical man, after all, and a Head of Security always found a way. 'We'll go through her bags,' he said with resolution. 'Don't leave until I've told you she's clean.'

Alone in the study, Natasha looked at her watch. The fire was dying down and it was nearly forty-five minutes since Kazim had left her. She heard several voices. Footsteps ran upstairs and then down again. Doors banged.

Once she thought she heard Kazim and went to the study door. But when she opened it, the hallway was empty. In fact, she had the oddest feeling that until she had opened that door there had been three or four people outside it, all pointing what looked like television remote-control devices at various spots on the walls.

She shook her head and closed the door. 'Now you're seeing things that aren't there,' she told herself. 'You need to get home and get your head straight, Natasha.'

But there was no sign of Kazim, and Kazim was her only way out of Serenata Place. So she went back and put another log on the fire and tried to concentrate on whatever bits of the Sunday papers she could find.

It was several logs later when he eventually came into the study.

'Sorry to keep you waiting,' he said, as if it had been a few minutes instead of a couple of hours. 'There are still a couple of administrative matters that need my attention. You must be hungry. I'll have tea sent in. What would you like?'

'To get home,' said Natasha. 'Maybe I could try one of the local taxi firms again?'

'No need,' he said firmly. 'It really won't take much longer.'

But instead of going about whatever it was he had to do, he sat down opposite her, picked up the telephone on a side table, and dialled a single number.

'Tom, Ms Lambert's anxious to get home. I've told her I won't be long, but meanwhile send in some tea and sandwiches, will you, please?' He put the phone down and smiled at her. 'It's been a long time since that splendid brunch of yours. You must be hungry. You'll feel better after some food.'

'I feel fine now,' Natasha told him wearily. 'I'd just like to get home. I have a lot of work to do and an early start tomorrow.'

But he just went on smiling.

She said pleasantly, 'Why do I feel like Bluebeard's last wife?'

He jumped and the smile slipped a bit. 'What?'

'As if there's something going on here you don't want me to see, but you're not going to let me go in case I have,' explained Natasha matter-of-factly.

The smile disappeared altogether. 'Why do you say that?'

Her eyes narrowed. 'And why don't you deny it?'

He considered her for a long moment, the dark eyes thoughtful.

'How can I deny it?' he said softly. 'If that is what you feel, it's what you feel. There's nothing I can do about it.'

Natasha met his eyes. He was not being straight with her. She was certain of it. Yet he was not telling absolute lies either.

She said slowly, 'You're very clever, aren't you?'

His expression did not change, but she had the impression that it was not the answer he wanted.

He laughed gently. 'Is that a coded way of saying you dislike me?'

'It's a coded way of saying I don't trust you,' said Natasha with brutal honesty.

But even that didn't disconcert him. 'Alas,' he mourned. 'And you have been so perceptive about my character up to now.'

With a deliberate movement he sat back in the winged chair and crossed one leg over the other. He put one perfectly manicured hand on his knee and Natasha remembered that whiff of expensive cologne she had caught when he'd been showing her to her room yesterday.

She knew what the whole pose was telling her. And he was right. How could she ever have been stupid enough to think this exquisitely turned-out man was a butler? She frowned quickly and looked away, embarrassed.

'That was not fair of me,' he said lightly. 'You are too much of a delight to tease. Forgive me.'

But Natasha did not think he had been teasing. Or that he had been particularly enjoying himself, either. Carefully ignoring his plea for forgiveness, she said slowly, 'What do you do, Kazim? When you're not teasing unwary strangers, that is?'

He waved one of those beautiful, long-fingered hands. 'Oh, I negotiate deals,' he said vaguely.

'I'll just bet you're good at it,' said Natasha with feeling. No mean negotiator herself, she felt as if she'd gone ten rounds with an expert.

The firm lips twitched. 'You're very kind. But it is dull stuff for the most part. Not interesting to anyone else. Tell me instead about your own work. Now that I find very interesting.'

'Really?' She was sceptical and did not try to disguise it.

'Really. What is involved in market research? Are you one of those people who accost me in airports with clipboards wanting to know which bottled water I drink?'

It would be a brave interviewer who approached Kazim al Saraq, thought Natasha mordantly. She said so.

He looked put out. 'I am not approachable?'

'You are—' She bit it off before she got too personal. Instead she shrugged. 'No, what you're talking about is the raw material for quantitative market research. That's all about numbers and market share. It's mainly done by statisticians. Numbers people.'

'You are not a numbers person, then?'

Natasha detected patronising. She curbed her dislike. If she wasn't nice to him, she might never get out of here, she reasoned.

So she said evenly, 'I can work with them when I need to. But my speciality is what is called qualitative market research. It is more about interpretation—detecting changing tastes before they happen; trying out new products in different markets.'

'Focus groups,' he deduced. The disdain was evident.

Natasha sighed. She had met this attitude before. 'Focus groups have their place, of course. They're not the whole answer, though. Someone like me is only as good as her interpretation of what the focus groups say.'

'You mean you spy on people,' he said. It sounded like an accusation.

Natasha raised her eyebrows. This was a new one. 'I don't spy on private conversations.'

He looked at her hard. 'Don't you?'

Natasha frowned. This was more than a general dislike of market research. This sounded serious.

But before she could demand an explanation, the study door opened and a man appeared at it with a large tray.

'Tea at last,' said Kazim with evident relief. 'Thank you, Tom.'

The man set the tray down, but here was another mystery,

Natasha found. He was not any more convincing a butler than Kazim had been. He was ever so slightly clumsy with the tray—and when he gave her a cup of tea and offered the plate of sandwiches, he looked at her much more searchingly than a well-trained servant would normally do.

What on earth was going on? Natasha was beginning to be alarmed.

'The car is ready,' the manservant told Kazim. 'You can leave as soon as you want.'

'Thank you, Tom.'

Natasha gulped her tea. 'Then let's go now. I'll just do a last-minute check of my room, and see you in the hall.'

Was it her imagination, or did the two men exchange glances in consternation? Natasha didn't care. Against the odds, it seemed, she was going to get out of Serenata Place tonight. She hurried upstairs and ran a practised eye round the room. No forgotten sweater…no dirty lingerie under the bed…no make-up in the bathroom… *Dirty!*

'My shoes,' she said and ran downstairs. She had dropped them in the boot cupboard after she had retrieved them from the garden. They were probably irreparable. But she didn't want to leave anything of hers behind in this creepy place.

Both men were waiting in the hall, talking seriously, apparently absorbed in their conversation. But she could feel their eyes on her as she dived into the boot cupboard. And when she emerged with the shoes, the manservant had whisked them away from her before she knew what was happening.

'What are these?' he said, more like an interrogator than a butler. And then as they smeared his immaculate hand, 'They're filthy.'

Natasha thought the mud stains served him right. She only wished they had ended up on Kazim.

'They're a very expensive pair of high concept shoes which I—er—lost in the garden when I arrived,' she said crisply. She glared at Kazim.

'My fault, no doubt,' he said smoothly. 'More apologies. You must leave them with Tom and he will do what he can to restore them. Or if he cannot, of course, I will replace them.'

Natasha did not like that at all. She did not want to leave any trace of her presence in Serenata Place.

'There's no need for that,' she said, grabbing quickly at the shoes.

But Tom moved out of range even more quickly.

And Kazim was smiling that caressing, deceptive smile again, saying, 'But I insist.'

There was nothing she could do.

They swept out through the gates—operated electronically this time—and he took them with rapid efficiency through hedged lanes and minor roads. He was driving well enough, but he was frowning and Natasha did not think the road had all of his attention. The car, though, was the last word in silent luxury. She stretched her long legs out in front of her and gave herself up to thought.

He did not speak until they got onto the motorway. And when he did, it was so unexpected she nearly slid off the comfortable seat in astonishment.

'Who let you back into Serenata Place this morning?'

She shook her head, not understanding him. 'Let me back?'

He clicked his tongue. 'After your shopping expedition. Who opened the gates to let in that car?'

She chuckled. 'Oh, it was the old cigarette-packet trick.'

It was his turn to look blank. 'Cigarette packet?'

'Haven't you ever seen that on film? To stop a burglar alarm ringing, you put a cigarette packet between the hammer and the bell. I did that to stop the gates locking. Well, I used a branch, actually. I don't smoke. But it worked just as well. When we came back I just had to push them.'

'Just had to push…' He sounded stupefied.

'The simplest solutions are always the best.' She could not keep the smugness out of her voice. 'I always tell my clients that.'

It seemed he could not speak.

Natasha turned slightly in her seat and looked at him curiously. 'Something wrong?'

'Not at all,' he said in a strangled voice. 'You are an education.'

He pressed a button on the dash and said into the air, 'You can stop worrying about how they overrode the gate controls. I've found out what happened.'

A ghostly voice came out of the speakers. 'Have you found the transmitter they used? We really need that.'

'No transmitter.' Kazim didn't sound strangled any more. In fact there was a note of unholy laughter in his voice now. 'It was all much more low-tech than that.'

The voice was affronted. 'Low-tech? It can't have been!'

'I assure you it was. One of my guests opened the gates manually, then propped them open with a branch.'

The voice began to swear with feeling.

Kazim glanced sideways. His lips twitched.

'She's with me in the car.'

The voice stopped abruptly.

'And I shall be taking her home, Tom. I'll call you with my revised ETA.'

He flicked the switch.

A horrible silence filled the car. Natasha was not used to being in the wrong. She didn't like it.

At last she said in a small voice, 'I messed up, didn't I?'

'Just a bit,' agreed Kazim.

Another, longer silence.

'I'm sorry.' She meant it, genuinely. Yet it came out like a sulky schoolgirl. Natasha could have screamed with irritation.

'Forget it. Now we know what happened everyone can relax.'

But Natasha was too honest to let it go at that. 'I really am sorry. I should have thought. If you have electronic gates, it's because you want to keep people out of the place.'

'That's one way of putting it,' agreed Kazim dryly.

'And I had no right to ignore that. I apologise. I really do.'

He sent her a more genuinely friendly smile than she had yet received from him.

'Thank you. But don't beat yourself up about it. It was good practice for my Head of Security.'

'You're very kind,' said Natasha stiffly, still smarting under the sting of conscience.

He shrugged. 'Hey, these things happen.'

But she was too mortified to reply.

In the end he stopped trying to converse and concentrated on the busy road. It was only as they approached London that he asked for her address.

Natasha told him. Her flat was in a mansion block right in the centre of Mayfair, with a swimming pool and heavily carpeted corridors, thick with discretion. So discreet, indeed, that it did not even have an identifying plate on the door.

Not so discreet—or so expensive—that Kazim did not know it.

'Oh, there,' he said. 'One of my aunts had an apartment there for a while. Convenient, of course. But isn't it a bit middle-aged for a cool chick like you?'

Natasha promptly stopped feeling conscience-stricken and went back to loathing him cordially. It was a relief.

'I am not a chick.'

One eyebrow flicked up.

She said in a goaded voice, 'And I find the block very comfortable.'

He chuckled. 'You're full of surprises.'

'I'll take that as a compliment,' said Natasha, bristling.

'You should,' he said, astonishing her. 'Frankly it's a long time since a woman surprised me.'

There was a pregnant pause.

'And it's a long time since I've heard a man say something like that,' she said in a conversational tone. 'In fact, I think it's a first for me.'

He was unperturbed. 'So I've broadened your experience.'

'Oh, you have.' She was sweetness itself. 'Who would guess that I could bump into a dinosaur in broad daylight?'

'Dinosaur?' He was astounded.

'Macho dinosaur,' said Natasha, in case he missed the point.

He sounded bemused. 'No one has ever called me that before.'

'Then they should have.' She recognised the road they were travelling along. 'Left here, then right, then a quarter left,' she instructed him curtly.

He followed the instructions meekly.

'Drop me at the front entrance. The car park has a full-time attendant. They don't let people in unless I tell them in advance,' began Natasha.

But he was already turning down the dark little side street and edging the big car up to the protective grille.

'Now you'll have to back out or do a ninety-five-point turn,' said Natasha. Not without satisfaction.

But, to her amazement, when he pressed the electronic button to lower the driver's window the grille and barrier were already rising.

'Good evening, Your Highness,' said the intercom. 'Nice to have you with us again, sir.'

'Good evening, Hicks. I'm not staying. Just seeing Ms Lambert to her apartment.'

'Good evening, Ms Lambert.'

'Good evening,' said Natasha in a muted voice. She was beginning to feel badly outclassed.

Kazim drove in and parked the car so close to the doors to the lift lobby that it was clear he had been here many times before.

He got out and came swiftly round to help her, pausing only to take her case out of the back.

But Natasha was too quick for him. She swung herself out of the door before he had the chance to offer his hand.

'Thank you. Very efficient. Right to the door.'

'Not quite to the door yet.'

'But quite far enough,' said Natasha firmly. She almost snatched her case from him.

His eyebrows rose. 'You're very anxious to get rid of me.'

'Not at all,' said Natasha primly and untruthfully. 'I just don't want to be any more trouble. Goodbye.'

He ignored that. Calmly he took the case back from her before she realised what he was doing and strode to the door to the lift hall.

Eyes narrowed to slits, Natasha pattered after him. He stopped and held the door open for her. Was there the slightest hint of mockery in the courteous gesture? She stopped too, glaring.

'Is this where you tell me it's no trouble?' she challenged.

He smiled down at her as if he was enjoying himself enormously.

'Let's just say, I pay my debts.'

She was utterly bewildered. 'What debts?'

'Well, it's down to me that you lost your phone with the number of your car service. So it was up to me to make up for it.'

'And that's all? That's the reason you've driven me all the way here?'

'What other reason could there be?'

Their eyes met. His eyes were brown and guileless, limpid with honesty. She didn't trust him an inch.

'I just wanted to show you my human side,' he said gravely.

She knew he was laughing at her. She just couldn't prove it. There was a moment when the air crackled with antagonism. And then she pushed past him.

'Oh, you've done that all right,' muttered Natasha, stomping up to the lift and punching the button for all she was worth.

Kazim followed.

'Now what's wrong?' he asked patiently.

Natasha was so mad with him, she actually told the truth. Well, part of the truth. 'Do you know how long I've lived here?'

He blinked at this change of tack. 'Er—no. Should I?'

She did not wait for an answer. 'Three years. Three—

damned—years. It was my present to myself when I realised the business was going to be a success.'

'Well done,' he said, still evidently puzzled.

'And in three years, I have never disentangled one porter from another,' Natasha said furiously. 'Still less found out their names.'

'Ah.'

'And you remember which one is Hicks. From his *voice?* When you don't even live here?'

'A memory for names goes with the job,' said Kazim apologetically. And waited.

Natasha even saw him waiting. She knew she was supposed to say, 'What job?' or even, 'Don't tell me you work!' And then ask him up to her flat and they could carry on fighting. He seemed to enjoy it.

But she had had enough. Ever since they'd met, he had needled her and teased her and put her in the wrong. And he had won every bout. Natasha wasn't a sore loser, but she had had enough defeat this weekend to last a good long time.

She turned to face him and stuck out her hand.

Her tone was final. 'Thank you for driving me home. And thank you for your hospitality.' Her eyes gleamed momentarily. 'However reluctant.'

And then, at last and too late, he did look a little uncomfortable. He took her hand and held onto it.

'For that, at least, I think I perhaps owe you an apology.' It was said with a rueful charm that Natasha was a hundred per cent certain was contrived.

'Oh?' she said distantly.

'You see, Isabel was very upset when you did not arrive on Friday, as you promised. I am afraid I jumped to the conclusion that you just could not be bothered to come—or to let her know. I realise now that I was at fault.'

'Don't apologise,' said Natasha with her falsest smile. 'I'd so much rather go on loathing you without feeling guilty about it.'

He blinked. 'Loathing me?' he echoed, as if he thought she

was joking. It was obvious that nobody had ever said that to him before. Suddenly there was not a thing about his demeanour that was contrived. He was utterly spontaneous—and mad as a hornet.

'Oh, certainly,' said Natasha, pleased. 'Almost from the moment we met. In fact, I think it would be a good idea if we didn't meet again.'

Kazim's spine was very straight. 'If that's what you wish, of course.'

'I'm quite sure it's mutual,' said Natasha, still smiling.

No more hammer thumps of the heart, she thought. No more being looked at as if she were an unwanted pizza delivery boy. No more electric touch. And no more being laughed at. And no more of that heart-stopping lust that looked like honesty.

Sounded good.

He gave her a chilly bow. 'Then goodbye for the last time.'

'Hold that thought,' she said.

CHAPTER SEVEN

NATASHA'S apartment had never looked more welcoming. No Gothic towers, no Egyptian bathrooms, she thought. Just simple polished floors, pale furniture, and big spaces. Uncluttered comfort, that was what she liked.

So why did it look bleak, all of a sudden? For the first time ever, she saw her home as antiseptic. Empty, even.

'Grrr,' said Natasha.

She had no hesitation in laying the blame fair and square where it belonged. On the handsome shoulders of Kazim al Saraq.

'Who is about as homey as a polar bear. You are out of your tiny mind, girl!'

She pulled all the cushions off the chairs and sofa and made herself a nest on the Chinese rug in front of the fire. It felt good. All the while she had been in Kazim's house, she had felt his presence, as if he were watching her. Here she was free, she told herself. Here she was answerable to no one.

Except that she didn't feel free. She felt as if someone had slipped a rope round her ankles while she wasn't looking and now she could not move.

'You can move,' she said between her teeth. 'Nobody ropes you.'

She had a long bath and then curled up among the cushions with a crime novel. But the story failed to hold her. Every five minutes she looked up, as if she were expecting the phone to ring.

It was crazy. Very few people had her phone number. Even fewer called her on a Sunday night. They knew it was her private time. So—why?

She tried listening to music. But restlessness kept intervening.

She kept thinking of all the sharp, smart things she should have said to Kazim al Saraq when she'd had the chance.

And she kept remembering that smooth golden chest and the level, amused eyes. Particularly the eyes. As if he thought she fancied him.

She ground her teeth—and went and had another bath, watching some television programme on the Roman Empire from the scented water.

'This,' she told herself, with reluctant amusement, 'is the pits. Get a grip, for heaven's sake. You've got a heavy week coming.'

But for once work had no appeal. She leafed through her New York files without enthusiasm. She didn't seem to be able to take in more than a sentence here and there.

'Pull yourself together, Natasha Lambert. This is your livelihood. Besides, you love it.'

Only suddenly it was boring. She wanted to be back arguing with Kazim al Saraq. Only this time she wanted to *win.*

She thought about the way he had looked at her, all the way down that arrogant nose. Oh, he had decided to be mischievous and charming later. All that prowling round her in the kitchen! No doubt he thought all of that was great fun! But underneath the charm he was an autocrat to his cold, cold heart.

Men like that didn't let anyone else win. Ever. Especially not a woman.

'So don't waste your time,' she advised herself.

She put on her velvet robe and made herself some cocoa.

'Gosh, that's a throwback,' she said, struck, as she stirred the rich, creamy liquid. 'I haven't done this since I was at school. Pure comfort food. Damn! I shouldn't need comfort after one dodgy weekend!'

She clutched it to her breast as she wandered round the flat. She had always loved its high ceilings, and great curved sweep of sitting room that overlooked the river. Now it didn't feel spacious. It echoed.

'Listen, one run-in with Machismo Inc is *not* going to turn you into Doris Day,' she told herself firmly. 'That is definitely not the way you want your life to go.'

But he's gorgeous.

Yes, sure, he's gorgeous. That golden skin would look wonderful against her pale cushions...

She found she was mentally arranging him on the sofa and taking his clothes off. It brought her back down to earth with a thump.

'If you want to date, date,' she told herself severely. 'But don't start dreaming fairy tales. You know better than that.'

For you didn't date men like Kazim al Saraq. Even Natasha, loathing the arrogance and despising the machismo, knew that. You fell in love—infatuation—whatever you wanted to call it. The Kazims of the world sat back and let you worship them. And that was exactly what you did.

'Not me, baby,' Natasha told her reflection. 'Never have. Never will.'

Kazim got slowly back into the Jaguar. His brow was furrowed and it was a moment before he switched on the engine.

Not meet again? She couldn't be serious.

But she had sounded serious. More than serious. Hostile.

'Well, that's a new one,' he said aloud.

In his experience women were never hostile to a man who was both rich and royal. But then Natasha Lambert was an original in every sense of the word.

'You haven't got time for this,' his responsible, intelligent self told him.

'I'll make time.'

'And she doesn't want to see you again.'

'I'll change that.'

'She thinks you're a dinosaur,' his prudent side reminded him.

'Then I'll have to make her fall in love with dinosaurs. Heck, it's been done before.'

Fall in love?

It stopped him for a microsecond. Who had time to fall in love? Then he shifted his shoulders. Well, something like that.

He looked at his watch. Time he checked in with Security. Tom would be starting to worry.

He cruised gently out of the car park, raising a hand to the CCTV cameras in acknowledgement of the porter as the barrier rose.

At once, his phone started to beep. He put it on loud speaker again.

'Kazim here. I'm east of Park Lane and south of Oxford Street. I'll be at the residence in five minutes.'

'Taken Cinderella home, then?' said Tom acidly. Between failure of state-of-the-art electronic security systems and the British Special Branch, he had had a bad evening.

'Yup.'

'You do realise what a risk the woman is?'

Kazim's lips twitched. 'Oh, I do. A blonde who bites.'

'This is not funny, Kazim. We know nothing about the woman. She could be anyone.'

Kazim swung the steering wheel. 'Sure.'

'Well, I hope this is the last you see of her.'

'That makes two of you.'

Tom was not listening. 'She's just too big a risk,' he said in a scolding tone.

And quite suddenly Kazim laughed aloud. 'Sorry, Tom,' he said, with relish. 'Some risks a man just has to take.'

By five a.m. Natasha had stopped even trying to sleep. She got up and dressed. Outside, the sodium lights were eerie in the deserted streets. It was very cold. A lone car swished past, its lights making rainbows out of the spray it sent up. Natasha shivered and huddled her coat collar round her throat.

Kazim al Saraq should see her now, she thought grimly, then caught herself. Why keep thinking about the man? Surely she had more control than that.

A cruising cab appeared. It was showing a 'For Hire' light. Thank God, thought Natasha, and raised her arm.

The office was a blessed relief. At least she had never pictured Kazim al Saraq naked on her desk! Also, there was plenty to catch up on, after her week in New York.

Her deputy, Leo Duvallier, found her at her desk with a pile of completed files in front of her when he arrived at eight-thirty.

'Ah. The frenzy of the in-box,' he said, shaking out his wet umbrella and hanging it on an old-fashioned coat stand that Natasha kept because it reminded her of her first job. 'Found anything frightful yet?'

Natasha looked up, her eyes narrowing. 'Should I have done?'

Leo shifted uncomfortably. He was fast and perceptive, which was why she had appointed him, but he was not long on diplomacy.

'Jason Turville has been blasting away a bit. I told him you'd handle it when you got back.'

Turville was the head of a major advertising company, with subsidiaries worldwide. Natasha frowned.

'Why?'

Leo was disarmingly frank. 'Well, you know me. I would only lose my head if he started ranting at me.'

'I mean, why is he ranting?' said Natasha, with patience.

Leo pulled a face. 'Search me. I stopped listening after ten minutes.'

'Ten minutes, eh?' Natasha was impressed. 'He *is* mad. I suppose he's heard that our report rubbished his last ad campaign for David Frankel.'

She picked up the phone.

Leo was fascinated. 'You're going to call him?'

'No point in putting it off.'

'You want to be careful. He was spitting tin-tacks.'

Natasha thought of Kazim al Saraq and grinned to herself. 'Wow, something new, for a change.'

'You—are—dangerous,' said Leo, admiring. 'I'm a pacifist. I can't bear to listen. I'm going to get coffee.'

He was wise. Jason Turville was very angry indeed—and voluble. Natasha was still listening when Leo returned from his trip to the coffee shop.

He put a tall waxed cardboard cup in front of her. Natasha, feet on desk, phone under her ear, thanked him with her eyes. As he sat down she swung her feet to the floor, with decision.

Then she switched the conversation onto broadcast so Turville's fury rang round the office, and began calmly to prise the plastic lid off the coffee-cup. She sipped appreciatively.

'Three more minutes,' she mouthed at Leo. And raised three fingers so they could silently count the minutes down together.

At the end of three minutes, she quite simply took charge. Interrupting the flow of invective, she said mildly, 'Jason, are you serious? You can't be mad at me for doing my job.'

Jason Turville, international advertising shark, was sufficiently astonished to skid to a halt mid-rant.

Natasha pursued her advantage ruthlessly. 'Frankel asked us to review the product worldwide, from introduction to the present day. There was no way we could ignore the advertising.'

'That campaign won prizes,' said Turville, beginning to steam again.

'Sure,' said Natasha crisply. 'The industry loved it. Very artistic. Very subtle. The target market hadn't got a clue what you were on about. That campaign bombed. David Frankel showed me their sales figures.'

Sounds of inarticulate rage filled the room. Natasha stayed cool.

'Sorry, Justin. The punters aren't postmodern enough for you. Better luck next time.'

She cut the call before he could find words.

'Wow,' said Leo, half amused, half horrified. 'There's another man who hates you. You surely are building a mailing list, aren't you?'

Natasha was taken aback. *You're a difficult woman,* Kazim al Saraq said in her head suddenly. She winced.

Leo did not see it. 'Oh, well, like you always say, we get paid to tell the truth, not win popularity contests.'

'I say the cleverest things,' said Natasha wryly.

But she was unsettled. So when Izzy rang, she seized the phone gratefully.

'I won't have it,' said Kazim, sweeping into his office that morning without ceremony. He was in full desert robes, in preparation

for a formal lunch at a charitable foundation. His face was like
thunder.

Martin looked up, startled. 'What?'

'Women. Loathing me.'

'First I've heard of it,' said his personal assistant peacefully.
'Er—are you sure? What time do you want the car to pick you
up?'

'I'll call when I'm ready. The meeting may go on into the
evening. I want to convince them to send a delegation to the
reconciliation meeting.'

Kazim waved the delicate negotiations aside. 'As for loathing—I had it straight from the source.' He glared at the file
Martin was holding out. 'I am a dinosaur, apparently.'

His personal assistant could not avoid a quick look at the
formal photograph of the Emir on the wall behind the desk. The
hawklike profiles were startlingly alike. He stared at Kazim in
horrified fascination.

'Some woman has called you a dinosaur?' he said gropingly.

Kazim took the file without glancing at it and threw it into
his monogrammed briefcase. 'Isn't that what I just said?'

'She can't have meant it,' the assistant said from the heart.

'She meant it.' Kazim was grim.

'What on earth did you do? Throw her up across your horse
and gallop her off into the desert?' He glanced at the big chart
of Kazim's schedule pinned to the wall behind Kazim's head.
'Er—make that the Home Counties.' He gave a small choke. He
controlled it manfully.

Kazim flung himself back in the antique chair behind the in-
laid desk that had been his one personal indulgence when he'd
set up the Paris base.

'Go on, laugh,' he said moodily.

Martin Page shook his head. In public he meticulously re-
ferred to Kazim as His Eminence and never a word of criticism
passed his lips. In private, however, Kazim asked for the un-
edited truth—and got it.

He got it now. 'It's been a long time coming.'

Kazim's head reared up in shock. 'What?'

Martin was crisp. 'Welcome to the real world.'

'What are you talking about?'

'Real relationships are work.' Martin's voice was neutral. 'Most of us don't get away with sweeping out on a wave of international diplomacy, tossing a diamond bracelet behind us as we go.'

He eyed him warily. But Kazim was not offended. An eyebrow quirked. 'Bitter, Martin?'

'Envious,' said Martin with feeling. 'Nice to see you having to walk the same tightrope as the rest of us for once.'

'You're taking her side?' Kazim said in mock indignation.

Martin smiled. 'So it's got to sides now, has it? Wow. Who is this discriminating woman?'

Kazim snorted. 'Discriminating! That's the last thing she is.'

'Then you've got nothing to worry about, have you?'

'No, but—' Kazim broke off as he realised what Martin had said. 'You mean if she'll date anyone, she'll date me too? You're nearly as insulting as she is.'

His outrage was definitely pretend. But in spite of the wry self-mockery, there was something at the back of his eyes that was deadly serious.

Martin shook his head, disbelieving. Kazim was never serious about women.

Kazim got up restlessly and paced about the room, his robes flowing. He seemed lost in thought. A frown creased the strong black brows.

Martin watched him. This was not like Kazim at all. Clearly he had to be needled out of this introspection.

'So when are you going to see the girl again?'

Kazim did not stop his pacing. But it did bring him out of his preoccupation.

'See her again?' He glared. 'You can't be serious.'

Martin pursed his lips. But he said nothing.

'Why should I want to see her again? The woman insulted me!'

'Maybe that's why. Don't you want to make her eat her words?'

That brought Kazim up short. His eyes narrowed. 'That sounds like revenge.'

Martin was the picture of innocence. 'Make her fall in love with you...then cast her aside like a worn out glove,' he suggested in a thrilling voice.

There was a seething silence. Martin watched him warily. Kazim was clearly contemplating physical violence.

In the end he opted for heavy sarcasm, instead. 'Oh, yes, very traditional. You think I'm as much a dinosaur as she does,' he accused.

Martin kept a straight face, but only just. 'Not a dinosaur,' he demurred. 'Maybe a little set in your ways.'

'Set in my—' Kazim was speechless.

Martin couldn't hold it any longer. He bubbled over.

'Oh, Lord, you should see your face,' he said when he could speak.

Kazim grinned reluctantly. 'Thank you very much for your support,' he said dryly.

Martin went over to him and slapped him on the back.

'You don't need support. You need a crash course in handling the Twenty-first-century Ferocious Female.'

Kazim looked all the way down his haughty nose, disdainful as a hawk in the desert. 'I don't think so.'

Martin was disappointed. 'Oh, well, you're probably right. You haven't got the time for personal complications until the reconciliation conference is over.'

'You misunderstand me.' Kazim's eyes glinted. Suddenly he was a hawk about to fall on its prey. 'I don't want a crash course.'

'Er—no?' asked Martin, confused.

'No.' Kazim's mouth took on a line that made him look very like the autocrat on the wall behind him. 'I want it to take as long as it takes. As long as it would take you. Or Tom. Or any other man on my staff.'

'Sorry?'

'You've convinced me. I'm going to work this one out on my own.'

Martin was now completely lost. 'Huh?'

Kazim gave him a bland smile. 'Ferocious Female, vintage twenty-first century, versus Desert Dinosaur. Where will you put your money?'

Natasha and Izzy agreed to meet for lunch in windswept Soho Square. Izzy was already in the gardens when Natasha arrived. It had stopped raining and the November sunshine was brilliant through the leafless trees.

'I should have brought my sunglasses,' Natasha remarked, half closing her eyes against the glare.

'Cold, though.' Izzy was wearing vibrant woollen mittens, but she still rubbed her hands together like a Dickensian orphan. 'What are the sandwiches?'

'Smoked salmon or avocado and bacon.'

'I'll take one of each.'

Natasha divided the food and they chomped companionably as they paced through the twiggy garden.

'Okay,' said Izzy. 'What do you want?'

'What?'

'Come off it, Natasha. You're busy, busy. I can never get time with you. And now we get together twice in two days? How come?'

Natasha looked away.

'Or can I guess?' said Izzy suddenly. 'You locked horns with Kazim al Saraq and now you want to know all about him.'

Natasha strove with herself. 'He was vile to me when I arrived. He ordered me around like I was his slave. And he never told me he owned the damned manor house until it was much, much too late.'

'Too late for what?'

'My cool,' snapped Natasha, remembering a little too clearly. She could feel the heat in her face all over again.

Izzy's eyes popped. 'Your ears have gone pink.'

'What do you expect out here in the wind?' Natasha sat down on a bench, and Izzy joined her.

'So you don't want his phone number?'

Natasha was disdainful. 'Why on earth would I want his phone number?'

'You could always call him up and ask for a date,' murmured Izzy mischievously.

Natasha shuddered before she could stop herself.

Izzy was all innocence. 'But why not? You've called guys for a date before, I know.'

Not guys like Kazim al Saraq.

Izzy warmed to her theme. 'It would be good for him. Show him that the modern woman can take the initiative.'

Natasha glared at her. 'I may be a modern woman. I'm not a masochist.'

'Well, I'm disappointed,' said Izzy naughtily. 'I thought you were the one truly independent woman I knew. I never thought you'd let what other people think get in the way of doing what you want.'

'I don't want to date Kazim al Saraq,' yelled Natasha.

Izzy laughed until she choked.

Moodily, Natasha threw some crumbs of her unwanted sandwich at a couple of sparrows, then stamped her feet and yelled at marauding pigeons who saw a chance to get in on the act. The sparrows seized their chance and took off with their booty. Natasha sat back, satisfied.

Izzy stopped laughing. She looked at Natasha under her eyelashes. 'Kazim is Dom's best friend, you know.'

'Oh?' She could not have sounded less interested. She bent to pick up the plastic sandwich pack.

'They climb mountains together,' Izzy told Natasha's stooping form.

'Oh.'

'He comes across as a bit of an unreconstructed male supremacist, I know. But he's a good guy really,' urged Izzy.

'Mmm?'

'At home, he's some sort of prince,' said Izzy, trying hard. 'That gives him loads of responsibilities. Dom says he finds it very difficult sometimes.'

Finds responsibility difficult? *Kazim?* Izzy didn't know what she was talking about. The man would just love ordering people around!

Natasha did not say so, but her restraint made her twitch badly. 'Hurrumph.'

Izzy gave up. She started talking about her wedding instead. But very soon Natasha realised that Izzy kept trying to nerve herself to say something and then veering away at the last moment.

'Let's get out of this wind,' said Natasha, and walked her friend briskly to their favourite Italian coffee shop. Once they were seated and the son of the proprietor had brought them two steaming mugs, she said casually, 'So what is happening at your wedding that you haven't plucked up courage to tell me yet?'

'You know me too well,' Izzy said.

'You're not used to being deceitful.' Natasha's smile was crooked. 'I am. I know the signs.'

Izzy fished in her bag for a handkerchief. 'I wish you wouldn't put yourself down all the time,' she said, blowing her nose.

'And I wish you'd stop hedging. What's the bad news?' A thought occurred to Natasha. Briefly a look of horror touched her perfect features. 'You're not expecting me to wear blue tulle?'

Izzy choked. 'No, no, it's nothing like that.'

'Well, what, then?'

Izzy drew a deep breath. 'It's—um—the walking down the aisle bit—'

'I'm not making it a double wedding,' Natasha said firmly. 'I love your father to bits but he's not my type.'

Izzy smiled, but absently. 'It's Kazim,' she said, not very coherently but with great resolution.

Natasha was not surprised. 'Ah.'

Izzy drew a deep breath. 'He's Dom's oldest friend. Dom's asked him to be best man. I know you didn't like him, but neither of you was at your best when you met. It's only for one day and he can be very nice…' Her voice tailed away under Natasha's ironic gaze.

There was a difficult silence.

Izzy's shoulders slumped. Some of her bright energy dimmed. She had not been looking forward to breaking the news to Natasha. And it was turning out even harder than she had feared.

Dom had said lightly that Natasha and Kazim would be friends once they had a chance to get to know each other, but Izzy knew it wasn't going to happen.

Not that Natasha was a man hater. She liked men's company. She made no secret of it. Izzy knew she had affairs, though Natasha said frankly that none of them was important enough for her to introduce the man in question to her closest friend. Men, said Natasha, were good entertainment but not a sound long-term investment. Izzy was sure there had been some deeply wounding relationship in her friend's past. But whenever she asked, Natasha just laughed and changed the subject.

Izzy never argued, though it never seemed to her that the casual affairs made her friend happy. But Natasha said they left her in control and that was the only way a woman could protect herself.

Sheikh Kazim, thought Izzy now with a flash of comprehension, would never let a woman take control. Or anyone else for that matter. Maybe that was why he made Natasha bristle the way he did.

She was saying now, 'Kazim al Saraq may be many things. But *nice* he definitely isn't.'

Izzy sighed. 'Please don't fight with him, Tash. The wedding is going to be difficult enough.'

This was news to Natasha. She frowned. 'Difficult how?'

'Oh, Dom's family. They're all lords and dukes and have huge houses and horses and things. My mother might have coped if she were still alive, but my father—well, he's not a natural wedding organiser. And Dom's stepmother never misses a chance to put me down.'

Natasha's blonde head reared up like a war horse hearing trumpets. 'What?' she said incredulously. 'And Dom *lets* her?'

'He's not there most of the time,' pointed out Izzy. 'He's off training. And bloody Janine takes me off for what she calls a girls' lunch and makes me feel as if my underwear is not up to her standards.'

Natasha ground her teeth. 'Bitch.'

Gentle Izzy did not disagree. She sighed. 'But she's in charge of his family's side of the wedding. And she's got my father running scared. That's why I—' She hesitated.

This was clearly the thing she had been trying to nerve herself to say all through lunch.

'That's why you—?' prompted Natasha.

'That's why I was hoping you could take her on,' said Izzy in a rush. 'I know it's not part of the chief bridesmaid's duties. But you go ten rounds with captains of industry. You can handle Janine.'

'I can,' agreed Natasha. 'So what is the downside?'

'What?' Izzy was all innocence.

Suspicious innocence, in Natasha's judgement.

'Well, as you dislike Kazim so much, I just wondered whether you would mind having to liaise with him over the wedding arrangements.'

Natasha stared at her, silenced.

'Best man and chief bridesmaid,' Izzy went on, gabbling. 'They have to work together. And, of course, he has to escort you out of the church.'

Natasha groaned from the depths of her soul. But she didn't say she wouldn't do it.

Izzy realised it was going to be all right after all. She leaned forward and gave her friend's hand a comforting pat. 'You'll be fine. You're a star, Tash.'

'I know,' said Natasha gloomily.

'And you *will* be civilised to Kazim if he walks you out of the church?'

Natasha chuckled. It was her turn to lean forward with a comforting pat on the hand. 'Put it this way, I won't *start* a fight.'

Izzy had to be content with that. From her expression it did not look as if she found it reassuring.

*   *   *

When Natasha got back to the office she found Leo contemplating a package on her desk with deep fascination.

He looked up when she came in. 'How come you're getting free mobile phones these days? Why doesn't it ever happen to me?'

Natasha stared. 'Free—?'

She tore at the wrappings. Inside, sure enough, was the slimmest, most gleaming little cell phone she had ever seen.

Leo whistled. 'Hell. That's platinum.'

Natasha almost dropped the thing.

'Careful,' said Leo, shocked at such negligence. He fielded the phone.

Natasha was scrabbling through boxes and packaging like a terrier at a rabbit hole. 'When did it come? Who brought it?' she said over her shoulder.

'That's another odd thing,' said Leo, perching on the corner of her desk and twirling the little phone. 'He looked like a banker, talked like a robot and was clearly a shoe fetishist.'

That startled her so much, she even stopped scrabbling for a moment. '*What?*'

'Wanted to give it to you in person. When I said you weren't here, and I didn't know whether you'd be back today, he wouldn't give it to me. Prowled round your desk a couple of times before he could bring himself to put it down. And when he'd gone your I'm-in-charge shoes had moved.'

Natasha blinked. She kept a complete change of clothes at the office, in readiness for unexpected meetings. What Leo called her I'm-in-charge shoes were Chastity Fair originals with four-inch heels and ankle straps. They lived under her desk. Only now they were against the wall.

'I'd say he'd been sniffing them,' said Leo with relish.

'Don't be ridiculous.' But Natasha was shaken.

Leo leaned sideways suddenly and flicked up a business card she had missed.

'Kazim al Saraq,' he read aloud. He turned the little slip of pasteboard over. '"I told you I pay my debts."' He looked up. 'What debts?'

'Nothing,' said Natasha. 'A misunderstanding.'

Leo stared at her narrowly. 'Are you blushing?'

'Don't be ridiculous,' snapped Natasha. She dived behind her desk and made a great business of putting her spare pair of shoes back in their normal place. When she straightened, it was not surprising that her cheeks were a bit flushed.

'You are,' crowed Leo, undeterred. 'Well, well, well. I've never heard of a man who could make Natasha Lambert blush before.'

She sucked her teeth and held onto her temper. 'And you haven't now.'

'So who is this Kazim guy? Someone you met in New York?'

'A friend of a friend's new fiancé,' she said calmly. 'I've only met him once. And neither of us wants to repeat the experience.'

She was wrong there too.

Kazim's lunch with the working party went on for hours, as he'd expected. In the end, he got to his feet.

'Thank you, ladies and gentlemen. We don't seem to have got any further forward from last time we met. So I think the time has come to stop double guessing the combatants and invite them to sit round a table. Please will you draw up a list of ways and means?'

He left while they were still wringing their hands and protesting.

He described the scene to Sir Philip Hardesty, down the phone line in New York.

'Yes, but what did their report actually say?' asked Philip.

Kazim was impatient. 'Predictable stuff. We shouldn't do anything yet. It's too soon. Too dangerous. You know the sort of thing.'

'They may have a point, though,' said Philip, the professional.

'Oh, not you too.'

'I just want you to be careful, Kazim. The world can't afford to lose you.'

There was a pause. Then, 'I'll be careful,' Kazim promised, sobered.

Philip's voice warmed. 'Try, anyway. I know all the security stuff is a pain. But, remember, you're a scarce resource.'

'Maybe. But somebody has to do it.'

Philip did not argue with that. 'At least let me talk to our international security contacts. You can delay for forty-eight hours, can't you? Go and brush up your real tennis or something.'

Kazim gave a great shout of laughter. 'Oh, I can think of something to pass the time that's a lot more fun than tennis.'

'Then do it. And I'll get back to you with the word in the souk.'

'It's a deal.'

Kazim was still chuckling as he rang off.

Martin put his head round the door. 'Well?'

Kazim threw himself back in the chair and stretched his arms above his head. 'Two days' delay while Philip Hardesty taps his sources.'

'Tom will be relieved. And you can give yourself a nice time in Paris for once.'

'Oh, I'm postponing Paris too.'

Martin was puzzled. 'Really? Why?'

'I'm staying in London.' Kazim was bland. 'Got a Ferocious Female to negotiate with. And while I think about it, get me the number of that lifestyle journalist who interviewed me in the summer. I need some inside information.'

By ten o'clock on Tuesday morning, Natasha had shifted the whole of the accumulated in-box. Which was just as well as she had a heavy meeting at eleven. Leo came too, for once, and the two of them were grilled exhaustively by the global CEO of a high-tech company. They didn't get back to the office until seven at night.

The receptionist of the building was not pleased. There had been a steady stream of callers, she said, pointedly. Some of them had been less than polite.

'We'll have to employ someone else if this goes on,' said

Leo, groaning as he slapped a heavy pile of response folders down on his desk.

Natasha skimmed her briefcase across the room. It landed neatly in the middle of her desk.

'Definitely not,' she said. 'I don't trust anyone else.'

'Surprise me,' muttered Leo.

Natasha gave a little superstitious shiver. 'We're only as good as our last report.'

'We're all as good as our last report,' said Leo, not very comfortingly.

They had had a tough day. Her blouse had shed a button in the course of the meeting and Leo's wrists were swollen from pounding the keyboard to support her presentation. Now Natasha shrugged out of her crumpled jacket and hung it over the back of her chair. 'Do you want a drink? I'm buying.'

'You mean will I stay late and work through the new version of the report with you,' interpreted Leo. 'You are so transparent.'

Natasha blew him a kiss. 'I love you too.'

The door opened and Kazim al Saraq walked in.

Natasha stopped dead, her hand halfway from her lips, as if someone had blown cryogenic ice over her. She seemed to have lost all power of speech.

It was left to Leo to handle the situation. After one quick, startled look at Natasha, he went forward with a winning smile.

'May I help you?'

'No,' said Kazim grimly.

Leo looked at Natasha for guidance.

She pulled herself together. Well, a bit.

'Um—this is unexpected.'

'I called,' said Kazim austerely. 'Several times. No one came back to me.'

He sounded outraged. It had clearly never happened before. Natasha's eyes narrowed.

'Sorry about that,' she said unconvincingly. 'My meeting overran.'

'Really?' he said, as if he didn't believe a word of it. 'And you hadn't allowed for that?'

Natasha set her teeth. But she said as cordially as she could manage, 'They added to the team unexpectedly.'

He looked down his nose. 'Surely you could deal with that. I thought you were such a hotshot professional,' he said maliciously.

That stung. 'Don't your meetings ever overrun?' Natasha flashed.

'Never. I keep control of them.'

Natasha blinked. Her sense of humour reasserted itself for a moment. 'Then you wouldn't get many contracts if you were doing my job.'

'It is simply a matter of management.'

Natasha was startled into a snort of laughter. 'Oh, sure. I can just see me managing David Frankel.'

That gave him pause, she was pleased to see. 'Frankel of Continuum?'

'Yup,' she said with satisfaction. That would make the superior bastard reassess her place in the business universe!

But it didn't. He was simply incredulous. 'You .work for Continuum Consolidated?'

Natasha stiffened. 'I don't work *for* anyone,' she said frostily. 'Continuum hire me when they need my expertise and my judgement.'

He was unconvinced. 'What expertise would that be?'

Leo, hitherto silent, gave a gasp of disbelief. It was some comfort. Natasha sent him a quick grateful smile, before squaring up to Kazim al Saraq.

'I,' she said with quiet satisfaction, 'am one of the top three independent market researchers in the world.'

Kazim said nothing. He watched her, unblinking. She could not tell whether he was impressed or not. Or whether he even believed her.

He looked round their small, minimalist office. Took in the subtle lighting and the absence of files. And his eyebrows rose in disbelief.

Leo moaned. He had been with Natasha when prospective clients had looked like that. Even when she was at her best, it usually earned a tongue-lashing that took several layers of skin off the perpetrator. And tonight she was tired and ratty, definitely not at her best.

'Natasha—' Leo said warningly.

She ignored him. Instead she drew herself up to her full height and leaned forward, glaring straight into the visitor's eyes. 'Believe me, I'm expert. And very, very expensive.'

Kazim gave a snort of laughter. 'Expensive, I believe.'

Natasha breathed hard. A little voice in her head was reminding her to stay cool. This man's blood brother is going to marry your best friend. You can't afford to brain him with a briefcase. No matter how much he deserves it.

Her eyes glittered. 'My work on changing preferences gets taught at business schools.'

But even that didn't impress him.

'"Changing preferences,"' he mocked. 'How much do you think people really change, Ms Lambert? They want what they've always wanted: to keep themselves and their family safe; have enough to eat; shelter from the storm. It doesn't take much research to work that out.'

Leo looked round for an escape route. Unfortunately, the handsome stranger was between him and the door.

But, uncharacteristically, Natasha was neither screaming nor throwing things.

'Today's consumer has a more subtle agenda.'

'Subtle!' Kazim said with disgust.

She gave him a wide, sweet smile and said with relish, 'Oh absolutely. I'm afraid your analysis is a little unsophisticated in today's markets.'

There was a disbelieving silence. Leo sank into the chair behind his desk and dropped his head into his hands. Natasha ignored him.

I bet no one's ever called Kazim al Saraq unsophisticated before, she thought. She could have danced with glee. She didn't.

He sent her a measuring look.

She was bland. 'It's a pretty complex discipline,' she said in a kindly tone. 'I dare say you haven't come across it before.'

And waited with pleasure for the explosion.

It did not come.

'You—' He bit off whatever he had been going to say. 'I think you like to wind people up, Ms Lambert.'

'Me?' Natasha was genuinely indignant. 'Don't be ridiculous.'

'Well, to be honest, Natasha—' began Leo.

Two pairs of eyes flamed him into silence.

She made an expansive gesture. 'Okay, I don't always dress things up prettily…'

'So I see,' said Kazim severely. His eyes fixed on the gaping blouse where she had lost her button, and stayed there.

Natasha followed his eyes and gulped. She could feel the heat in her cheeks. Damn! Glaring, she pulled the two sides of material together. Like some palpitating Regency miss, she thought, furious with herself.

She set her jaw and tried to will the blush to subside. 'Was there something you wanted? I'm afraid this isn't a very good time for us.'

'I can see that too,' snapped Kazim. He looked intensely at Leo.

'I—er—think I'll look at this stuff at home,' said Leo cravenly. 'See you tomorrow, Natasha.'

He pushed round the visitor and scrambled out of the door, still pushing one arm into the sleeve of his overcoat as he went.

'I'm taking you to dinner,' announced Kazim, before the door had barely closed.

Natasha stared at him in disbelief. 'You're joking.'

'Not at all. I cancelled an evening in Paris to take you to dinner.'

He gave her a slow smile. It was as if he had undergone a character change the moment they were alone. He seemed to have forgotten that she had ever annoyed him.

Natasha looked at him with deep suspicion. 'Am I supposed to be flattered?'

'Certainly. It's a one-off.'

'Really? Well, here's another one.' She was so angry she could barely speak. 'I never go out with strangers.'

'I so agree.' His look was full of spurious sympathy. 'That's why I spent some time researching you last night.'

'You did *what?*'

'On the Internet. I didn't even ask my assistant. I did it personally. You should be flattered at that too.'

Natasha closed her eyes. 'You're unbelievable.'

'No, no,' he said, deliberately misunderstanding her. 'I don't grudge a moment.'

'Get out,' she said, between her teeth. 'You're smug, arrogant and terminally not my type. Please leave.'

He gave her an odiously smug smile.

'Interesting, isn't it? It's a first for me too.'

'I will not—' began Natasha with fury. She skidded to a halt. 'Too?' she echoed, in quite a different tone.

He did not answer that. 'I've booked a table for eight-thirty. You will want to go home and change.'

Natasha surveyed him for a smouldering moment. 'You,' she informed him, 'are very high-handed. Has anyone ever told you that?'

His eyes glinted. 'If you mean I know my own mind and am not afraid to take decisions, I take that as a compliment.'

She ground her teeth. 'I did not mean it as a compliment.'

'That's what makes it all the more flattering,' he assured her outrageously.

He gave her a sudden blinding smile. 'Don't fight me on this one, Natasha,' he said softly. 'I've only got a few hours.'

There was something in the way he said it. It almost sounded as if he were like Izzy's Dom, going off into the dangerous unknown. It gave her pause.

Natasha pulled herself together. 'I suppose you think I'm going to melt at your feet in a puddle of gratitude?' But her heart wasn't in it.

'That would be a waste,' he murmured.

Natasha blinked. His eyes were warm. *Warm.*

He was impossibly dictatorial. He had the nose of a Roman

emperor and he wasn't ashamed to look down it. And he was much, much too tall. But his eyes…

Okay, it could have been some more of his diabolical teasing. Or the world-class manipulation. But, somehow she didn't think it was.

She said abruptly, 'Give me ten minutes.'

CHAPTER EIGHT

NATASHA kept a change of underwear at the office, along with an elaborate sequinned jacket. The jacket was fun rather than elegant, but it had got her through more than one cocktail party. She did not have a clean blouse. But her underwear drawer gave up a velvet basque that had done sterling work at a teen-magazine disco.

So—if Kazim al Saraq could face being seen with a racy party girl, then he could take her out to dinner. And if he didn't like it, then she would *know* that the warmth in his eyes had been deliberate deception.

She whisked into the small cloakroom and hastily changed into the evening finery. Then she looked at herself in the mirror and despaired. Nothing could hide the expert cut of her blonde hair, but it looked dusty and lifeless. There was not much she could do about that now, nor the shadows of weariness under her eyes, she thought. She shrugged. Oh, well, this was not the first time she had had to go on the town straight from work and she could make a reasonable fist of it, if she tried.

Concentrating, she brushed subtle colours onto her eyelids with swift, practised strokes. Then she darkened her lashes, blotted her skin and dashed matt foundation and a glimmery silk powder over it. A touch of blusher to highlight her cheekbones, a carefully chosen crimson to make her mouth look voluptuous, and she was ready.

Or nearly ready. She hesitated over the shoes. But then something in her said, 'Go on. If you're going to be a party girl, be it *right*.' So she dug out the high, high heels with sexy ankle straps. And then she really was ready for anything.

Kazim took in the transformation without expression.

'I don't need to go home to change. If you want to take me out to dinner, this is how I come.' It was a blatant challenge.

'So I see.'

He strolled over to her and parted the technicolor jacket. The basque gave her a spectacular cleavage.

'That top is verging on the illegal.'

Natasha put her head on one side. 'Are you complaining?'

He shook his head slowly. Very slowly.

'Thought not,' said Natasha.

She caught up her briefcase and led the way out of the office, head high.

Kazim, she thought wryly, had come out of the first round this evening a whole lot better than she had. Sure, she had made a good stab at style, done her best with paint and glitter, but anyone who looked closely would see how artificial it was. Whereas Kazim was the real thing.

He was wearing another of his well-cut dark suits with a blindingly white shirt. Platinum gleamed discreetly at his cuffs. His tie was silk, of course, a shadowy design of grey and silver. The contrast with golden brown skin was stunning. Natasha had no doubt at all that he knew it. He gave off a scent of clean laundry and shoe polish and that expensive cologne. And he looked gorgeous.

I am not going to feel outclassed, Natasha vowed silently as she got into his car for the second time in her life. He's doing it deliberately. I am not going to let him get to me.

She held onto her briefcase like a talisman.

He took her to a restaurant that she had heard of but never visited.

'Bankers,' she said, eyeing its discreet frontage with a professional eye. 'Amazingly good food that costs an arm and a leg. Full of expense accounts.' She was obscurely disappointed.

'You don't want to eat here,' he said acutely.

She shrugged. 'Well, it's not exactly the sort of intimate place I generally go on a first date. But I have no doubt the soufflé is to die for.'

His eyes flickered. At once she could have kicked herself. A first date, for heaven's sake? A *date?* She sounded like an adolescent. Worse, an adolescent hungry for his attention. Ouch!

But they did not go into the main dining room, with its expense buzz and tables full of suits nearly as beautiful as his own. Instead, they were shown upstairs and ushered into a small, beautifully furnished room.

So he was not going to let the world see that they were together, even for a couple of hours! It was like a blow to the stomach.

Kazim gave soft-voiced instructions, which she did not catch. Pulling her jacket across her challenging cleavage, Natasha wandered round the small room. She tried to forget the insult and concentrate on the prints on the walls.

An impassive waiter came in, bringing pre-dinner drinks. Natasha turned from contemplating a black and white drawing of a geisha. The Japanese beauty had folded hands and her eyes were downcast. Presumably that was the attitude Kazim looked for in a woman, thought Natasha grimly.

Kazim indicated her and the waiter padded silently across to her, as submissive as the geisha. He presented her with a tall glass of something pink and fizzing. Then he offered the other glass, full of ice and a slice of lime, to Kazim. He went. The door closed behind him with hardly a sound.

'A chaise-longue exit if ever I saw one,' said Natasha, her voice a little too loud.

She tried hard to be amused. But, to her surprise, it sent a little pain to her heart too. She was sophisticated enough to recognise what all these elaborate preparations meant. Kazim wanted to take her to dinner, sure. He just did not want them to be seen together in public.

Kazim raised his eyebrows at her over the top of his glass. 'What's a chaise-longue exit?'

'The butler tiptoes out, so as not to break the mood. The master then tumbles the chorus girl on the chaise longue,' she said crisply. 'French literature is full of it.'

He paused in the act of raising his glass to her. 'You must have read some very odd French literature.'

He was looking at her with a half smile, as if just looking at her was pleasure enough. If it was a trick, it was a good one, thought Natasha dispassionately. Most women would turn into pure marshmallow if he looked at them like that. She thanked God she was not most women.

She said coolly, 'No, pretty standard French literature, I believe. *Gigi* for a start.' She looked round at the red plush chairs and looped curtains. 'For instance, this is what they would call a *chambre séparée*.'

His eyes were watchful all of a sudden. 'Is it?'

'Yes. The sort of room where the dashing guards officers brought their mistresses.' Natasha paused. 'Or the girls they wanted to seduce.'

There was absolute silence in the little room. They stood measuring each other like duellists.

'Really?' he said at last, displeased.

'Really,' she echoed, mocking him.

'Surely, seduction is a very old-fashioned idea for a woman of the twenty-first century?'

She looked him up and down deliberately. 'It certainly is.'

This time the silence was like a stringed instrument, vibrating with tension.

'Do you think I brought you here to seduce you, then?' he said at last, very softly.

She met his eyes squarely. 'It seems a possibility.'

'You're very cool about it.'

Natasha shrugged. 'No skin off my nose.' She held his eyes deliberately. 'I don't seduce easy.'

Equally deliberate, he let his eyes drift down to her shadowed cleavage. The jacket had fallen open again.

'Then you like to play games.'

Natasha resisted the temptation to pull the jacket tight across her bosom. Instead she raised her glass to him in a mocking toast. 'Doesn't everyone?'

He looked interested, damn him. 'I thought you were too serious. Do tycoon businesswomen play games?'

'They do exactly what they want to do,' said Natasha with more bravado than truth.

He gave her a long, slow smile, intimate as a caress. 'I find that very encouraging.'

Natasha's pulses kicked into hyper drive on pure reflex. As no doubt they were supposed to. That look was high-octane sexual promise and he knew it, no question. *Careful,* she told herself.

She made herself relax and cast her eyes to the ceiling. 'You can stop smouldering at me. It doesn't do a thing for me.'

'Then you must tell me what does,' he said politely.

Natasha could have screamed. Instead she put down her drink, barely tasted, and sat down at the beautifully appointed table.

'I wouldn't want you to waste your time,' she said with her most charming smile.

He nodded, as if she had just issued a challenge. 'I'm grateful for the consideration,' he said, still polite.

She assimilated this. She was not sure she liked the implications.

'So what—you're not going to stop this charade?' The charm cracked a bit. '*Why?*'

Oh, he was smooth. 'You are delightfully modest. This charade, as you call it, is irresistible to any red-blooded male.'

Natasha was honestly puzzled. 'You mean you have to do the full desert-seducer bit, just because I tell you it's a waste of time?'

'Not entirely,' he murmured.

'Why, then? Am I a challenge of some sort? A worthy opponent? A new experience?'

'All of those.' He gave an odd little bow, like a duellist saluting his challenger. 'Also—a very beautiful woman.'

It silenced her.

Kazim gave her a bland smile and sat down opposite her. There were candles on the table and she saw the flames reflected in his eyes. It made him look as if he were laughing.

Natasha ground her teeth: sexy, smouldering and laughing. It wasn't fair.

He must have pressed a hidden bell because, as if by magic, the waiter returned with their first course. She gave a snort of dry amusement. Sexy, smouldering, laughing *and* in total control. Oh, boy, the dice were loaded against her.

His eyes flickered. 'What is it?'

'Private joke,' said Natasha. 'You wouldn't appreciate it.'

He didn't like that. Good!

She never remembered afterwards what they ate. If, indeed, she ate anything at all. She remembered him pouring wines, soft with the scents of France, harsh with the heat of summer. But she barely touched them either. He, she saw, did not drink anything but water.

He said, 'Our best friends are getting married. Isn't it time we called a truce?'

A truce with this laughing, self-confessed seducer? What a joke!

'Yes,' said Natasha, lying in her teeth. 'Let's be civilised.'

So food came and was removed and all the time they talked.

Talked about his work. 'I run the family charitable trusts. At least, I do in theory. In practice we have so many advisory boards, they more or less run themselves. These days I spend more of my time as an unofficial international mediator.'

She was surprised. And reluctantly impressed. 'Isn't that terribly difficult?'

'Oh, impossible. But people have to start talking some time. Somebody has to start it. It might just as well be me.'

She had asparagus on her plate at that point. She arranged it absorbedly, turning the spears to the points of the compass.

'Is it dangerous?'

Was it her imagination or did he withdraw slightly?

But his tone was light when he said, 'Only to the boredom threshold.'

She did not believe that. 'I mean—are you a target for extremists?'

Yes, definitely a withdrawal. His shoulders were tense as he shrugged. 'Who isn't? All you need is to be in the wrong place at the wrong time.'

She began to see that she had underestimated Kazim al Saraq. He might be more high-handed than was credible in the twenty-first century. And he might have a nasty taste for sexy teasing. But there was more to him than the macho dinosaur she had called him.

'I'm impressed,' she said simply. And meant it.

They talked too, about her life. Well, her company, but she claimed that was her life.

'Why market research?'

She shrugged. 'I'm good at reading people.'

He chuckled. 'You haven't been so good at reading me.'

Natasha let that pass. 'Okay. Groups of people. I'm not always so good with individuals.'

'I must remember that.' He leaned back in his chair, sipping sparkling water. His eyes didn't leave her face. 'How did you get into it?'

She gave a little spurt of laughter. 'Would you believe, standing on stations with a clipboard?'

'I thought you only did qualitative research? And that was altogether more upmarket.'

He was teasing, but his voice was warm again. It slid down Natasha's spine like gently heated treacle. She gave a little voluptuous shiver.

'You remember that?'

'I have a good memory for important things,' he agreed gravely.

Natasha, keep your head!

She still found herself giving him a suddenly shy smile. 'Flatterer.'

For a moment he was silent. Then he said slowly, 'No. That wasn't flattery. That was the truth.' He sounded surprised.

But she was shaking her head at him, laughing, disbelieving.

'You're right, of course. Numbers on their own don't tell you much. But still, that's how I started. I was desperate for a job and you don't need any qualifications to ask people what brand of soap they use.'

'No one's ever asked me what brand I use,' he complained.

She chuckled. 'That's probably because you're statistically insignificant.'

'What?' He was outraged.

Her eyes sparkled. She gave in to pure enjoyment. 'Do you buy your household supplies? No. You delegate it. The manufacturer will want to know what the purchaser takes off the shelf. Who buys the soap you use? Your housekeeper? Valet? Girlfriend? Wife?'

There was a little silence. Their eyes met. His inscrutable. Hers dancing.

He said slowly, 'If you want to know if I'm married, ask me.'

All the fun died out of her as if someone had pulled the plug.

'I don't,' she said sharply.

His eyes bored into hers. He was not hostile, but somehow—relentless. As if he was not going to let her off the hook until she told him the truth.

In the end, she looked away, with a shaken little laugh.

'Rich, powerful, handsome men tend to be married.'

'So ask,' he invited gently.

Natasha gritted her teeth. 'Are you married?' she said, as if it strangled her.

'No.'

Nothing more. She glared. But having come this far she saw no point in stopping there.

'Why not? Or are you going to tell me you've never found Miss Right?'

'Would you believe me if I did?'

'I'm too old to believe in fairy tales.'

His eyes glinted. 'Not a romantic, are you?'

'No,' she agreed with feeling.

'Want to tell me why?'

But she wriggled her shoulders as if to throw off something that was scratching at her and said, 'Answer my question first.'

'My single state? Okay.' He moved the salt cellar with great concentration. 'These days, I'm too busy. When I was younger—well, let us say, I didn't have much luck.'

Natasha stared. 'Luck?'

His mouth curled. 'I was jilted,' he said with complete sang-froid.

There was a moment of total silence.

Then—'I don't believe it,' said Natasha on pure reflex.

He laughed aloud at that. 'Thank you. But it's true. Forty-eight hours before the ceremony too. The social fallout was un-believable.'

Natasha would never have believed that she could feel any sympathy for this arrogant anachronism. But she found she wanted to lean forward and take his hand, comfort him.

Comfort Kazim al Saraq? She must be out of her mind!

She reached for irony. 'Believe me, it doesn't show.'

His eyes glinted. 'I'm glad to hear it. And you're quite right. If we had managed to marry, she would have bought the soap.'

Natasha expelled a long breath. Thank God she hadn't given into that momentary weakness. She put both her hands in her lap and clasped them together tight. They must not betray her and reach for him again.

Above the tablecloth, her smile was the last word in ironic sophistication. 'So why haven't you appointed an alternative soap purchaser since?' she asked lightly.

He laughed aloud and gave a little bow, as if he had met an opponent able to match him.

'My life is complicated,' he said with easy charm, dismissing the subject.

But Natasha was a twenty-first-century woman. Besides, she was used to dealing with charming evasions. 'Complicated in what way?'

He shrugged. 'Oh—I travel a lot,' he said largely.

'A wife couldn't travel with you?'

He looked horrified. 'I would never ask her to.'

Even a twenty-first-century woman was silenced by that.

After an awkward little pause, she said brightly, 'So where is your home, when you are not travelling?'

He was rueful. 'A good question. I have apartments in New York and Paris. A house here in London. Serenata Place, which you have seen. And a small tower by the sea in my own country.'

He smiled, as if just to think of it made him warm. It made Natasha like him a bit more. And liking, she knew, was a trap. She broke the eye contact swiftly and did not ask him about his tower by the sea.

'And you?' he said after a moment. 'Where is home to you?'

'I was born in a London suburb,' Natasha told him. 'My mother still lives there. I go back from time to time.'

He looked at her searchingly. 'Do you miss it?'

'No.'

'And now you live in an anonymous apartment block full of eighty-year-old duchesses,' he mused. He shook his head. 'So where is your spiritual home, Natasha Lambert? Downtown Manhattan or steamy jungle?'

Jungle! She flinched so hard that her chair juddered.

'Why do you say that?' she asked sharply.

He looked astonished. 'What did I say?'

Natasha could have kicked herself. There she went, overreacting again.

'Nothing. Forget it,' she said curtly. 'It's been a nice evening, but I ought to get back.'

She expected him to protest. Wasn't he supposed to be trying to seduce her, after all?

But all he did was nod politely and say, 'If you're sure?'

Natasha was surprised to find that she was disappointed. She hid it with a cheerful tone. 'I'm sure.'

'Then, of course, I will take you home.'

He got to his feet and held her chair for her. A waiter appeared. More of that control-freak magic, thought Natasha with irony. She decided that she wasn't a bit disappointed after all. Control freaks did not attract her.

Kazim was giving orders again. 'If you would call for my car, please, Michel.'

'At once, Your Excellency.'

The waiter disappeared. Kazim led the way downstairs.

Natasha looked at the back of his handsome head. 'But what about the bill?' she worriedly.

He waved a beautifully manicured hand. 'I never pay bills.'

'But—' She could not believe it. 'That's despicable,' she said hotly.

He turned round at that and looked up at her. His expression was unreadable. 'What a Puritan you are.'

'It's not exclusively Puritan to pay what you owe,' said Natasha hotly, fumbling in her bag for her own credit card. 'You do what you like. I'll go back and—'

His hand closed over her own. She felt that now-familiar little jump of electricity and looked up, meeting his eyes involuntarily. His expression was not unreadable any more. He was laughing openly.

'You are too easy to tease,' he said apologetically. 'The bill will go to my office. My assistant will pay it tomorrow morning. Come.'

He led the way out into the night.

Natasha followed, still torn. 'But—'

'I assure you, I do not cheat honest restaurateurs,' he said impatiently. 'I have been dining here ever since Michel opened his own business. He knows the way I do things.'

Natasha felt a prize fool. 'Well, lucky old Michel,' she muttered.

He laughed aloud at that. 'You know, you would find life easier if you occasionally gave me the benefit of the doubt,' he told her.

She glared.

And then three things happened simultaneously. Kazim's discreetly luxurious limousine glided to a halt in front of them; there was the sound of running feet, and Kazim seized her in a powerful grip and swung her round, so that she was between him and the wall of the restaurant, masked by his body.

A light flashed. Two. More. The feet ran off down a side alley.

The restaurant attendant leaped from the driving seat and

came round the car to them. 'Your Excellency, I am so sorry. I didn't see them. I—'

Kazim released Natasha and took the keys from him without a word. He opened the passenger door and almost thrust her into the seat. Then he rounded the car and leaped into the driving seat. The driver's door was barely closed as he took off.

Natasha struggled to sit up. 'What is happening?' She had lost a shoe and had to scrabble about among thick pile carpet to retrieve it.

Kazim looked down at her briefly. 'Probably paparazzi.'

'Oh.'

There it was again. That total resistance to being seen with her. It chilled Natasha to the bone.

'Don't worry. I can lose them if I have to.'

'I'm not worried,' said Natasha crisply. 'I don't care who photographs me. I haven't done anything I'm ashamed of.'

He did not answer. He was driving with controlled fury, skipping lights and sending the great car down alleys she would have sworn were too narrow for it.

Natasha sucked in her breath. 'And I just bet you don't pay speeding tickets, either.'

He did not answer. She saw that he was making a call on his cell phone.

She could not resist. She was too angry and, yes, too hurt. 'You do know that's illegal in this country?'

He ignored that too and spoke into the phone. 'Tom? Kazim here. They were waiting outside Michel's.'

A pause. Tom clearly asked a question.

'I don't know. They took photos.' Kazim's tone was matter-of-fact. But for some reason, Natasha sat bolt upright and turned to look at the road behind them.

Another pause.

'Myself and Ms Lambert. Yes, that's right. Lambert. My co-organiser of the Templeton-Burke wedding.'

Ouch, thought Natasha. *Co-organiser of the wedding.* That's me pigeonholed. How can I ever have thought it was a simple date? What a fool I am.

'I'll drop her off at her apartment and then meet you,' said Kazim finally. 'Half an hour maximum.' He cut the call.

Just as well I wasn't thinking of a long romantic good night, thought Natasha wryly.

When they arrived at her block, she smoothed her hair and said to the hard, handsome profile, 'Why don't you drop me at the front door? I know you're dying to be on your way.'

But he just shook his head, parked the car in a residents' bay and escorted her all the way up to the front door of her apartment.

It was only when he crossed the threshold that she remembered her uncomfortable evening on Sunday, with his imagined figure stretched out on her furniture. Naked, on her furniture.

She choked.

'Thank you. Er—good night,' she said hastily, avoiding his eyes.

She ground into silence when she realised that he was taking no notice at all. Instead she realised that he had brought a waxed carrier bag from the car, It was black and gold and he was now removing an oblong box from it. Neither bag nor box had any name on the side, but Natasha recognised serious shopping when she saw it.

'What on earth…?'

'I told you, you should give me the benefit of the doubt. I do pay my debts,' said Kazim al Saraq blandly. 'Always.'

With that, he whisked the lid off the box and presented it to her as if it were a crown. Natasha peered inside—and gasped. This was millionaire-class shopping!

The box contained shoes, each one tenderly wrapped in soft ivory velour. Natasha loved shoes. She knew that velour. Disbelieving, she lifted a corner of the material.

Something sparkled, bright as a dagger. Natasha dropped the velour and leaped back so fast, you would have thought the box held a rattlesnake.

'Those are Chastity Fair sunbursts,' she choked.

He beamed. 'I'm glad that they have found such a discerning owner.'

Natasha looked down at the Chastity Fair pumps she was actually wearing. They were sexy and gorgeous and they made her legs look a mile long. They were the most expensive shoes she had ever owned, at least five times the cost of anything else in her shoe cupboard. But they were not sunbursts.

The sunburst range was something the designer had brought out for Christmas. Natasha had read about it in *Elegance* magazine. It was a limited edition studded with real jewels. 'Something for the mega rich to bestow upon the woman he won't be spending Christmas with,' the magazine described them.

Gingerly, Natasha picked one out of its discreet ebony box. It was black suede, as soft as an eagle's wing, and across the toe there was a scatter of diamonds, like stars on a dark night. She stroked the shoe lovingly. It was beautiful, impractical and sinfully extravagant. More, it was the sort of thing a man gave to a woman he loved—or, as the magazine implied, a very rich man gave to a woman he did not care about one way or the other, but wanted to dazzle.

Natasha thrust it back in the box as if it had burned her.

'How dare you?' she shouted.

Kazim was bewildered. Right from the start, the evening had not gone as he had planned. She was too touchy. Too difficult. And much too combative. He never knew what she was going to say next. And now this volcanic reaction to a pair of shoes!

He frowned impatiently. 'My man did not report your size correctly?'

She blinked, as if the thought had never even occurred to her. Her eyes looked enormous and he realised with a little shock that they were magnified by tears. His brows snapped together. What was so wrong about the damned shoes that it brought tears to her eyes?

She swallowed and then said more quietly, 'I didn't mean to shout. Sorry. I must be more tired than I thought.'

'Then—'

'I meant, of course,' she said carefully, 'that I can't accept anything so—'

He looked down his nose. Here was her Puritan vulgarity

again. 'Expensive?' he said, on the faintest note of contempt. 'I assure you, these little pieces of nonsense mean nothing to me.'

Natasha gave a little nod, as if that was exactly what she expected. It irritated him deeply.

'But they might perhaps mean something to me,' she said almost inaudibly.

Kazim was still annoyed. 'What?'

She drew a deep breath and got her voice up a notch or two. 'I was going to say, I can't accept anything so personal.'

She put the lid back on the box and returned it to him, carefully. Her smile was lopsided.

'Or not unless it did mean something to me, anyway.'

He stared, all annoyance gone in sheer bewilderment.

'Which, of course, would be crazy. Utterly crazy.' It seemed to him that she squared her shoulders as if she were going to war. 'And now, I think, you really had better go.'

He did not know what to say, so he did not say anything.

Natasha blinked several times, rapidly, and almost thrust the box at him.

'Please. Thank you for the thought. But, no. And, please, I really would like you to go now.' Her voice rose.

Kazim saw the too-bright glitter of her eyes; the smile that she was having difficulty keeping in place; those shoulders, tense as if she were facing an enemy...

An enemy? What was going on here?

He took the box automatically, hardly glancing at it. He searched her face in disquiet. 'I never meant to distress you.'

'No. I'm sure you meant it kindly.'

He said, awkward as a boy, 'You lost your shoes in the shrubbery at Serenata Place. The least I could do was replace them.'

Natasha looked at him very straightly. 'But we both know that these shoes are a lot more than a replacement, don't we?'

'You are saying you will not accept a gift from me,' he said on a slow note of discovery.

Was her mouth shaking? He leaned forward to touch and she recoiled. He stopped dead, as if she had hit him.

Natasha drew a shaky breath. 'I am saying I will not accept a gift from you,' she agreed quietly.

It outraged him, but there was an odd little splinter of pain in there too. The pain astonished him so much he could not think of anything to say.

He saw her throat move. 'Now please will you go? I am very tired.'

In a flash of comprehension, Kazim thought, She wants me out before the tears start. It shocked him to the core. Who would have thought that such a simple gesture could go so horribly wrong? He would not have been surprised if she had flung the shoes back at him in anger. Scorn, even. He was fully prepared for scorn, given their earlier sparring.

But tears? Who would have imagined tiger businesswoman Natasha Lambert in tears? He could not believe it.

For the first time in years he was utterly at a loss. He had no idea what to do. So the simplest thing was to do what she said she wanted.

He went without a word.

The moment the door closed behind him Natasha sank onto the floor. She was shaking, right through to the centre of her body. It was a long time and half a world away since she had felt like this: confused; invaded; out of control. *In danger.*

All because a man had taken her out to dinner and chatted her up? And then tried to give her some wildly inappropriate shoes? It was ludicrous.

But it was also intense. Long after she went to bed and turned out the light, sleep did not come. Every time she closed her eyes, she saw Kazim. Every time she turned over, she heard him: his mocking laughter; his occasional disapproval; his imperious commands; his challenge.

He had not said it tonight, but it had been there, all the same, unspoken between them.

It would take me one night to change your mind. Just—one—night.

Natasha thumped the pillow with frustration. But in the end she gave in to wakefulness.

It went on for a week. In all that time to her relief—or so she told herself—she did not hear a word from Kazim al Saraq. Except for his regular appearance in her all too brief dreams, of course.

On the eighth night of near sleeplessness, Natasha took a policy decision.

'This,' she said aloud, 'has got to stop. Friendship or no friendship, Izzy is going to have to do without this bridesmaid.'

CHAPTER NINE

KAZIM prowled the magnificent rooms of the al Saraq palace, restless as a caged leopard.

'What's wrong?' Tom muttered to Martin.

'Campaign hit the buffers,' Martin hissed back.

Tom looked alarmed. 'The United Nations?'

'No, no,' soothed Martin. 'The Desert Dinosaur Campaign. Seems like the ferocious female won the first round.'

Tom grinned. 'Or maybe the second.'

Kazim was in full desert regalia for the summit meeting he was to chair in a few minutes. His white robe billowed as he paced. At the ninety-fifth turn, it swept a flurry of papers off a coffee table and onto the floor. Martin picked them up. Kazim did not notice.

Tom pursed his lips in silent whistle. 'She turned him down? That's got to be a new one,' he murmured.

They both looked at Kazim. Their sympathy was mixed with a certain wry satisfaction. Now at least he knew what it was like.

Kazim said, 'I want to know who took those pictures outside Michel's. How are we doing on that, Tom?'

Tom pulled out his organiser and tapped in a command. 'No one has offered them for sale.' He looked up. 'Maybe they're so fuzzy, they're worthless.'

'Maybe.' Kazim did not sound as if he believed it for a moment.

They looked at each other.

Tom sighed. 'Probably best if you don't date her again.'

Kazim frowned horribly.

'Tom means that you don't want to set up Ms Lambert as

125

someone you would pay ransom for,' said Martin hastily. 'That could put her in real danger.'

Kazim did not look at him. 'I know what Tom means.' His voice was harsh and he stared hard at his security adviser. 'He doesn't trust Natasha Lambert.'

Tom did not deny it.

Kazim picked the papers off the corner of the desk and flung them so hard at the opposite wall that they scattered like confetti.

The other two exchanged startled glances. They had never seen their controlled and courteous boss do anything remotely like that. There was a moment of frozen silence.

A muscle worked in Kazim's jaw. 'She returned my gift.'

That startled them too.

'Half the time she's interested—then suddenly she remembers something and she doesn't want to be in the same room with me.' It burst out of him as if he could not keep it in any more.

They watched him helplessly. Tom pursed his lips.

Kazim saw it. 'And, no, that doesn't mean she's an under-cover agent,' he snapped. 'It just means she's got a mind like a corkscrew.' He thrust an impatient hand through his hair. 'And now I can't even *talk* to her?'

Tom was astonished. 'You're going to take my advice?'

'Yes.' It was like a curse. 'What choice have I got? If I take her out again, I risk putting her in the spotlight of too many unpleasant people.'

It was so bleak that even prudent Tom was moved to offer a crumb of comfort. 'Well, you'll see her at the wedding.'

Kazim gave a bark of unamused laughter. 'If she doesn't get away first.'

Natasha rang Izzy to tell her that the bridesmaid deal was off. She had rehearsed it carefully. She even had notes in front of her. Point one: Izzy was too efficient to need backup from a friend.

But in Dom's absence his stepmother had invited Izzy to stay at the family home. 'For a training run over the wedding course,' said Izzy, shattered. 'Efficient? You should have seen me. I messed up big time.'

'Oh,' said Natasha, balked. She crossed out the first point. 'Still you can rely on Dom.'

'In theory. Only he's marching over the ice floes leaving me to handle the Wicked Witch of the Yorkshire Dales.'

Natasha scored through point two so hard she tore the paper. That only left the other potential bridesmaids. 'Well, you'll have all that family support behind you. Pepper and your sister and…'

'Jay Jay says she'll be abroad and can only make it back the day before the wedding. And now Pepper is pregnant and doesn't want to be a bridesmaid at all…' Izzy's voice rose and her laugh had an edge of hysteria.

Natasha crumpled up her list and lobbed it hard at the opposite wall.

But her voice stayed level. 'Okay. You've still got me. What can I do?'

Izzy hesitated. 'Would you come clothes shopping with me? I mean, if you have time.'

Natasha winced. 'Wouldn't Jay Jay be a better shopper's friend? Clothes are her business.'

'She's away,' said Izzy simply. 'And you're always so elegant.' She tried another of those terrible laughs. It wasn't any more successful this time. 'If I don't buy my dress soon, the stepmother-in-law from hell is going to take over that too. I just don't know where to start.'

On a tidal wave of sympathetic rage, Natasha forgot that she wanted to spend Izzy's wedding hiding under a big hat a long, long way from Kazim al Saraq. 'I do,' she said with energy. 'Stick with me, kid. We'll knock the woman *dead*.'

But when they looked at their diaries, it was impossible before Christmas. Natasha was deep in the madness of corporate pre-Christmas deadlines and Izzy's work was not much better. 'In the New Year,' they told each other.

Meanwhile, Natasha worked as if she were on rocket fuel.

'This time you've really lost the plot,' said Leo with gloomy satisfaction. 'We can't take on all this extra work. It's not humanly possible.'

But it was not only possible. It was essential if she was to get Kazim al Saraq out of her mind. For weeks, Natasha flitted between the office and back-to-back meetings. She averaged four hours' sleep a night. And, even so, every single time she walked into her flat she caught a hint of Amertage, the hush of a footfall behind a closing door, a warm breath against her exposed nape…

'Nonsense,' she told herself.

She filled the place with lavender-scented candles and left all the internal doors open. She even grew her hair to shoulder-length. It all helped a bit.

Between her housekeeping arrangements, the new hairstyle and work she got herself through to Christmas Eve without actually obsessing about Kazim al Saraq.

But then suddenly there was no work, London was empty and there was nothing she could do about it. Her mother was in South Africa for the winter. All her neighbours in the block had left to spend the holidays with friends or family. And suddenly the shadowy presence was not so easy to block out.

'I am going to enjoy the peace,' she announced to the empty flat, through gritted teeth. She pretended she did not hear the echo of mocking laughter.

She really had to work hard to keep Kazim's image at bay that day. As soon as she curled up on her old friend, the sofa, the first thing she thought of was that fantasy she had had the first time he'd brought her back home—Kazim reclining there, naked and utterly at home. She leaped up, scarlet-cheeked and spitting, and flung herself down on the rug.

She spent Christmas Day padding round her flat in a velvet robe and her pussy-cat slippers. But even the slippers weren't the comfort icons they had been before Kazim had raised his eyebrows at the sight of them in her overnight case. Damn him, how much of her life had he managed to touch?

She ate potato wedges, drank ice-cold champagne and listened to the whole of the radio adaptation of *The Lord of the Rings*.

Fourteen hours of hobbits, she reckoned, would effectively banish any lingering image of Kazim reclining on the sofa, with or without his clothes.

She was nearly right. Only then she went to bed.

The dreams started almost as soon as she closed her eyes. Sometimes she was alone on a beach. Sometimes she was in the midst of a crowded cocktail party. Suddenly a powerful figure flickered just at the edge of her vision. She turned to face him. And he was gone. But she knew who he was, all right.

Then she woke herself up calling his name.

Shocked, she lay there in the darkness. Her heart beat as hard as if she had been racing after him in reality instead of a dream. She was aware of a vast sense of loss.

Loss, yes. But hunger too. Natasha shot up from her pillow as she realised it. A shocking flash of desire lashed at her. How long since that had happened?

Never. Never like this.

Nowhere was safe from him: not her home, not her office, not her dreams!

It would take just one night…

She snapped on the light. 'What I need is more hobbits,' said Natasha grimly. 'And plenty of other bridesmaids to hide behind. Even if we have to get them from Rent a Body. I shall tell Izzy so.'

She rang her the next day. But Dom had mounted a surprise kidnap, descending on the Dare family home and whisking Izzy away for some romantic tramping over icy moors. By the time Izzy was back in circulation, Natasha had left for the USA. Then it was London Fashion Week and Izzy was working twenty-hour days.

In the end, they didn't get together until a cold bright spring day. By then Natasha had decided that she could keep a lid on the Kazim situation. He hadn't tried to contact her, after all. Her dreams were almost back to normal too. If she kept her head— and her distance—she could get through the wedding without making a total prat of herself.

Izzy too, was more hopeful. A week of Dom and the moors had done wonders for her self-confidence.

'I think it's going to be fun, after all,' she announced. 'Okay, my family are vile traitors. But you and me, we can handle anything. Even beastly stepmothers.'

Sexy dinosaurs? thought Natasha instinctively. She repressed the thought at once and produced a leather-bound notebook. 'Right. Let's start a To Do list.'

'Already got one.' Izzy whipped a much-folded sheet out of her bag.

Natasha scanned it fast. 'Dress, tick. Going-away outfit. Shoes. Underwear, question mark.' She looked up. 'Underwear *question mark?* Izzy Dare, are you telling me you mean to waft down the aisle with not a stitch under the ivory silk?'

Izzy looked pensive. 'It's a thought.'

'Hussy,' said Natasha admiringly.

Izzy chuckled. 'I'm working on it.'

Natasha surveyed her friend. 'You surely are,' she drawled.

Izzy's skin glowed and her brown eyes sparkled. Even the unruly auburn curls shone with life. Natasha compared her with the tense, scrawny woman she had known in the jungle and could hardly believe it. She said so.

'Love,' said Izzy with conviction.

Natasha looked away.

'You should try it sometime,' said Izzy gently.

A vision of Kazim, reclining on her sofa naked and laughing at her, whipped into Natasha's mind, unbidden. She flinched.

'Not all men are unreliable, you know.'

But that was a discussion she had never had with anyone, not even Izzy.

'Maybe.' Natasha banished the teasing image and hailed a passing taxi. 'We'll go to Odell's for your going-away outfit first. They might have something you like. If not, we can hit Sloane Street and do shoes at the same time.'

Izzy gave up.

The cab took them to a discreet house in an elegant terrace.

'This looks like someone's home,' said Izzy, hanging back,

suddenly diffident, but Natasha ignored her and strode up the shallow front steps and rang the bell.

'My friend the bride.' Natasha introduced Izzy with a flourish. 'She wants a going-away dress that will stun the opposition, impress the mother-in-law and make her husband want to take it off as soon as possible.'

'Tash!' protested Izzy faintly.

But Caro Odell was used to Natasha's forthright instructions. She nodded seriously.

'We can do that. Give me five minutes.'

In three she was back with a pot of fragrant coffee and some inspired ideas. It took less than an hour to find Izzy the perfect ensemble. Then Caro sent them to the right shops for matching shoes and some seriously alluring lingerie. By the time they emerged, Natasha and Izzy were giggling like schoolgirls.

But over tea at The Ritz later, Izzy lost some of her sparkle. She began to fiddle with a teaspoon and her eyes avoided Natasha's.

'Spill it out,' said Natasha, devouring cucumber sandwiches with a beatific expression. A sudden horrible thought struck her. 'If you want satin and frills, you're looking for a replacement bridesmaid.'

Izzy choked and dropped her teaspoon. 'Don't start me off again,' she begged. 'No, no, it's nothing like that.'

'What, then?'

'Well, it is bridesmaid stuff.' Izzy drew a deep breath. 'Er—um—walking down the aisle—'

'I walk in after you, keeping one hand free to take your flowers,' said Natasha, who had memorised her duties conscientiously. 'Follow you into the vestry to sign the register. Break out the lace handkerchief and the smelling salts in case you're overcome. Give you back your flowers and leave on your father's arm. Got it.'

Izzy smiled, but it was strained. 'Not my father, I'm afraid.'

Natasha stared at her. Another awful suspicion presented itself. This was worse, far worse, than frills. Suddenly The Ritz's delicious cucumber sandwich tasted of sawdust. She put it down.

132   IN THE ARMS OF THE SHEIKH

'What do you mean?' Her voice didn't sound like her own.

'Kazim is Dom's very oldest friend. Dom fingered him for best man almost before he asked me to marry him.' Izzy was gabbling. 'I know you two didn't get on, but neither of you was at your best when you met. It's only for one day and he can be very nice…' Her voice tailed away under Natasha's ironic gaze.

There was a difficult silence.

'Nice?'

'Well, he—he—he lent us Serenata Place for our party,' said Izzy defensively.

'*Nice?*'

'And he let us have fireworks.'

'And behaved as if he was prince of all he surveyed.'

Izzy shifted uncomfortably. 'Well, he is a sheikh. What can you expect?'

Natasha said in a still voice, 'What?'

'He's a bit old-fashioned about women, Dom says. But he can be very charming…'

'Did you say he was a *sheikh?*'

Izzy noticed that her friend was not following. 'Yes. So?'

Natasha closed her eyes. For a terrible moment she was back in that Hollywood Egyptian bathroom again, limping beside Kazim and trying to play nonchalant.

Everything but the sheikh. Oh, hell, she could even hear herself saying it.

Just as she could hear him saying, 'That could be arranged.' Oh, that wicked undertone. She'd *known* he was laughing at her, even then. She should have guessed he was a sheikh. Why hadn't she?

Sitting in a cream designer suit on one of The Ritz's civilised armchairs, with the scent of good coffee warring with French perfume, Natasha felt as if she had taken all her clothes off and danced naked round the discreetly luxurious room. She moaned.

'I wish I was dead.'

That brought Izzy up short. 'Tash?' She was worried. 'What is it?'

Natasha opened her eyes. 'He is a nasty, tricky, superior bastard,' she said, very precisely. 'He played me for a sucker from the moment we met. I do not trust him as far as I can see him.' And I see altogether too much of him in my dreams.

'Oh, is *that* all?' said Izzy, relieved. 'We're still talking about Kazim, I take it?'

'Who else?'

'You don't have to trust him.' Izzy was severely practical. 'You just have to walk down the aisle with him and smile for the cameras. Apart from that, you don't need to have a thing to do with Sheikh Kazim al Saraq. I promise.'

'Oh, sure,' said Natasha dryly.

She braced herself for an onslaught of invitations, diamond-studded shoes and serious wind-ups. And some X-rated dreams.

But, in fact, Izzy was right. Natasha did not hear a word from Kazim. After awhile she stopped jumping every time the phone rang. She assured herself she was relieved. Of course she was relieved.

Weeks went by. She and Izzy sent out the invitations, collated acceptances, talked to caterers and tried to keep last-minute hitches away from Dom's stepmother. Meanwhile, as Natasha pointed out dryly, the male half of the production was suspiciously silent.

On a crackly radio from the Arctic Circle, Dom said airily that there was nothing to worry about—Kazim had all the arrangements in hand. Kazim, wherever he was in the world, said nothing at all.

Relief gave way to serious annoyance. Annoyance turned into downright fury when Natasha realised that she was going to have to take the initiative to contact Kazim. It went against every principle and instinct. But Izzy was her best friend…

Grinding her teeth, she called his office. Once. Twice. No reply. She sent emails to his PA, which did not even get an automated acknowledgment. She told herself that it was only to be expected from a globe-trotting sheikh and tried to laugh. It still made her hopping mad.

First he bullied her; then he laughed at her; then he tried to seduce her with thousand-dollar shoes. Then four months of silence. The man was a walking insult to the modern woman. If he turned up in her dreams again, she was going to turn a fire hose on him!

Kazim shuttled between Europe, the Middle East and the Indian Ocean. Predictably, the reconciliation talks broke down again and again. Leaders squabbled, demanded sweeteners, were kicked out.

At a regional meeting, two local warlords pulled guns. Kazim rose to his feet and they stopped eyeballing each other while Tom quietly removed their weapons. But the international agencies decided talks were premature and shut up shop.

'So it's down to me now,' said Kazim. 'I don't have a board or insurance premiums to worry about.' Or a wife and family.

He took himself off for a wild, furious ride on his own. Then came back, said not a word of reproach to anyone, and simply started again, telling Martin to set up a series of bilateral meetings.

'Thank God for the private jet,' muttered Martin to Tom. 'Shall I tell Dominic Templeton-Burke to find another best man?'

But that Kazim would not hear of. They thought he said, 'I must have something.' It was so out of character, though, that each one of them decided he must have been mistaken.

Another thing, no matter how full his morning dossier was, the first thing he always looked at was Tom's report on Natasha Lambert. So when her emails finally caught up with them, Martin braced himself for fireworks.

'Sorry,' he said, coming clean. 'I guess the London office thought this was low priority.'

Kazim almost snatched the paper from him.

Natasha's reluctance to contact him shone through every word. He grinned for the first time in days. 'Better get her on the phone. At least she'll be glad to hear from me, after waiting so long.'

But Kazim did not get the welcome he expected.

Natasha was in a limousine, in transit between a presentation for a global cosmetic firm and the warehouse of a company that purported to provide portable cloakrooms for country-house wedding receptions. She was typing on her laptop with one hand and dialling Luxury Loos with the other. When Kazim's voice came through her earpiece she jumped and wiped out a whole paragraph.

'What do you want?' she snapped.

He was taken aback. 'I was under the impression that *you* wanted *me*.'

'Sheikh Kazim,' said Natasha dangerously, 'do not start trying to flirt with me now. I warn you, I am not in the mood.'

Sheikh? So someone had told her. She would not like that.

His smile widened, but he kept his voice bland as cream and twice as innocent. 'Flirting? I am responding to a message from you.'

'Oh, well, that makes all the difference.'

He was not deceived. 'What is wrong?'

'What is wrong,' said Natasha, very, very calmly, 'is that I asked you to call me a full fortnight ago. Since then, I've bought rings, organised the service, arranged transport and found the bridegroom's presents for the bridesmaids.' Her voice rose. 'Every single damned task that should have been yours.'

'I have been busy—'

She gave a small scream. 'Do you think I haven't? Do you think I am not busy now? I'm multitasking so fast, my fingers will fly off. Now get off the phone, you parasite and let me talk to someone who is actually some use.'

She cut the call so hard, she broke a fingernail. It still felt good.

Left staring blankly at his phone, Kazim began to laugh. While his assistants watched in disbelief, he laughed until he had to bend over to ease his aching ribs.

When he could speak he said, 'One more thing for the diary, Martin. Natasha Lambert wants to see me.'

Martin's eyebrows flew up too quickly for their owner to pretend.

It started Kazim off again. 'She may not want to admit it,' he agreed, choking. 'But she wants to see me very badly indeed. Set it up, will you?'

So that was how Natasha was sitting in her office at ten o' clock one night, running over a final draft of a report on bottled water, when she heard the swish of the lift doors on the landing.

Had Leo forgotten something? She rubbed her eyes, realising how tired and gritty they felt.

'Hi,' she said as the door opened. 'What did you—?' Her voice rasped to a halt.

He was there, leaning against the door jamb, watching her appreciatively. Large as life and twenty times as handsome, in his impeccable grey suit, with that half smile mocking her, as it always did.

She knew that look, the indefinable air of competence edged with danger. It stalked her dreams, making her angry, making her feel a fool, making her *yearn*.

'You!' spat Natasha, loathing her own weakness.

His lips twitched. 'Nice to see you too.' He unpropped himself and came quietly in, closing the door behind him. 'You look well.'

Sensing mockery, Natasha stuck her chin out. 'Oh, yes?'

She knew quite well that she looked frantic. She had been wrestling with the results of twenty separate focus groups since lunch. Her eyes had to be red from all that staring at the screen. She was hyped up on coffee and her hair, through which she ran her fingers constantly, had to be standing on end.

He strolled over to the desk. 'You've let your hair grow.'

She resisted the urge to pat it back into place and stood up. 'What are you doing here?'

He ignored that. 'I like it. It's pretty.'

'*Pretty!*' repeated Natasha with loathing.

He looked even more amused. 'You are the strangest woman. What's wrong with looking pretty?'

Natasha was crisp. 'Death to my street cred. So why did you say you were here?'

He looked wounded. 'I thought you wanted to see me.'

'Whatever gave you that idea?'

'But you sent me so many messages.'

'That was weeks ago. I could have used you then.'

He flung his arms out. 'And now I'm here. Use me.'

Natasha worked very hard at not thinking about her dreams or unwelcome astral visitors to her furniture. 'An email would have done.'

He was calm. 'Not for me.'

He rounded the desk and was suddenly much closer than she wanted. She stood her ground, but her eyes slid sideways, refusing to meet his glance.

He searched her face. 'You look tired.'

Natasha folded her lips together. 'That's the eighteen-hour days. I've got a lot of work on at the moment.'

He smiled as if he didn't believe her. 'I know that look. Can't sleep?' he asked softly.

Natasha set her teeth and stared hard at the painting behind his right shoulder. 'I know this may be difficult for you to get your head round,' she said with awful civility, 'but there's a direct correlation between the hours I work and my ability to pay the bills. I don't work, I don't eat.'

'It sounds as if you need someone to take care of you.'

She met his eyes then. 'I can't believe you just said that.'

Unabashed, he searched her face. 'Eighteen-hour days are crazy. There has to be a better solution.'

Her eyes flamed. 'I enjoy my work.'

'So do I. But I know I work better if I take a break occasionally.'

Now she was looking at him, she could see that the brown eyes were curiously intent. For once he did not seem to be laughing at her. It was a gentle look, almost caressing, as if he wanted to look into her very soul. Something from deep in her dreams stirred.

Careful.

'I have to take the work when it comes,' she said, but the fire had gone out of her.

'Sure. But you don't have to take everything that's offered, do you? I think you're using work to run away.'

'You're crazy,' Natasha said hoarsely.

He ignored that. 'I told you—I know that look. Want to know how?'

'No.'

He took no notice of that either. He came a step closer, another. She had to lean backwards slightly not to touch him. She caught a hint of Amertage again and the memories were like an assault. Oh, God, that smell would mean Kazim for the rest of her life. She could not drag her eyes away from his.

He said softly, 'Because I see it every morning in the mirror too. Dreams, huh?'

Kazim's lashes were amazingly long. How would they feel against her skin?

Natasha felt her whole body contract with longing. She bit down savagely on her lower lip.

His eyes darkened. 'Don't do that.'

There was a moment of total silence, like a spell. Natasha swallowed.

'Natasha—'

No, he was not laughing now. When he was laughing, she could just about resist him. Serious, he was lethal.

She stepped away. It was pure reflex. But it broke the spell.

'I wanted to talk to you about the wedding,' she hastily. 'Let me call up the file.'

She whipped into her seat and started stabbing inaccurately at the keyboard. Images of pie charts and adverts chased across the screen, bumping into each other. The machine beeped in protest.

Kazim was looking amused again. 'There's no rush.'

'Oh, believe me, there is,' said Natasha with feeling.

But she slowed down and found the file almost at once. She clicked on a couple of documents and the printer in the corner purred into life. She reached out for the pages and flicked through them to check everything was there. Satisfied, she stapled them together and handed them across with a flourish.

'This is what you want.'

He took the pages blankly. 'This—?'

'Arrangements.' She listed them, ticking them off on her fingers. 'Phone numbers, addresses, times. Key guests. Ushers. Izzy and I have done acceptances and where the guests are staying. All you have to do is look after Dom, pay the choir and make a speech.'

He made a slight movement, quickly stilled. She peered at him.

'You have prepared a speech?'

'I have it in hand,' said Kazim with dignity.

Natasha was certain that he had not even thought about it. And was equally certain that he was not going to admit it. For the first time since he had walked in, she grinned without reserve.

'Oh, I nearly forgot.' She rummaged through a desk drawer. 'The ring.'

He took the small velvet-covered box she held out to him across the desk.

'You're very efficient.' He sounded put out.

Natasha narrowed her eyes at him. 'Someone has to be.'

For a moment their eyes locked. Kazim drew a sharp breath.

'You don't think much of me,' he said at last on a note of discovery.

Natasha stood very still. As long as she kept on needling him, she didn't need to consider how his body would look without that suit. That meant that she didn't need to notice that he was thinner and, once you looked beyond the wicked twinkle, his eyes were strained. If she allowed herself to notice those things, then she would start feeling—and then she would be well and truly lost.

'I think,' she said carefully, 'that you're probably a great delegator. I just never asked to be delegated to.'

He gave a crow of laughter. 'How judgemental of you. You think I'm a dilettante best man.'

Natasha could have danced with rage. 'I don't think about you at all,' she told him crushingly.

Kazim grinned, clearly uncrushed. 'Ms Lambert, you're a bad liar.'

The effrontery of it almost took her breath away.

'I am an exceptionally good liar,' snapped Natasha, goaded beyond bearing.

His eyes danced. 'Is that a challenge?'

She began to feel harassed. 'Don't be ridiculous.' She looked at her watch.

His mouth was prim, but those eyes gave him away, as they always did. He was enjoying her discomfiture. 'Don't tell me. You want me to go so you can get back to work.'

That was exactly what she had intended. So Natasha was astonished to hear herself say, 'I don't think anything I did now would be any use. I'm wiped.'

He seemed surprised too. He raised his eyebrows. 'Then may I take you home?'

He clearly expected a rejection. Again she startled herself. 'Thank you. I'd be grateful.'

She logged off and locked up swiftly and led the way downstairs. Outside her building, Natasha shivered and pulled her smart jacket round her. It was not made to withstand the winds of March.

Kazim looked up at the night sky. 'There's hardly a star up there.'

The wind gusted again, whipping Natasha's hair across her mouth. She put up a hand to hold it in place, as she too blinked upwards.

'That's London for you,' she said lightly. 'Starlight is out.'

'Not just London,' he said enigmatically.

'What?'

'I have the feeling that starlight is not permitted anywhere in the Natasha Lambert universe.'

She made a rude noise.

He laughed softly. 'I could show you the stars, Natasha.'

'*What?*'

'You'd have to be a bit braver than you are at the moment, of course,' he murmured.

She knew deliberate provocation when she heard it. She cast her eyes to the cloud-covered and street-light-polluted sky and said, 'You're not only a dinosaur, you get your chat-up lines out of nineteen-thirties movies.'

'I'm glad that you can at least recognise a chat-up line. I was beginning to wonder.'

She swung round at that, hands on hips. 'Do your girlfriends normally fall for recycled movie dialogue?'

His eyes gleamed. 'My girlfriends fall for *me*. You're the first to complain about the script.'

It was too much. 'I am not your girlfriend,' Natasha shouted.

It echoed in the empty street. She felt a fool immediately. She had let him wind her up again! Another victory to the sheikh! Blast him.

Her shoulders slumped and tears of rage filled her eyes. To her horror, she found him holding out a snow-white handkerchief in silent sympathy. She knocked it away and dashed the tears away angrily.

'I never cry,' she said belligerently.

But for once he did not take advantage of his victory.

'I believe you,' he said, surprising her. 'It's not fair to tease you.' His tone was almost—if that had not been totally crazy—affectionate. 'You're out on your feet. And I have to admit that I have not been pulling my weight on this damned wedding. Come on. Home, with you.'

He gave her a maddeningly unreadable smile and opened the passenger door.

Natasha remembered that car. Her seat was like a feather bed. She sank back into it with a sigh of bliss as he got behind the wheel.

'Mmm.' She gave him the address drowsily.

'I know,' he reminded her. 'Why don't you go to sleep?'

'I'll be fine.'

But Natasha caught herself on an enormous yawn. Then shivered again.

Kazim reached one arm behind him and plucked a woollen rug, light and warm as a fairy cloak, from the back seat.

'Wrap that round you. The heating will be functioning in a minute.'

Oh, it was sweet to be cared for, Natasha thought. Even if it was by a man who had an autopilot programme for women who attracted him. She pulled the rug round her and her chin sank onto its frilled edge. She yawned again, massively.

'Stop fighting it,' Kazim instructed her, amused. 'I'll wake you when we get there.'

'I can't—'

But she did.

Kazim slipped through the central London traffic with the ease of long practice. He was amused to find that even the bright lights and honking horns of the Strand failed to wake Natasha. It also pricked his conscience. She must be exhausted—he had not realised how much stuff there was to do around a wedding. He should have listened to Tom and Martin when they had warned him. And he should never have left her to handle all that nonsense in addition to her own responsibilities.

What had she called him? A great delegator?

Well, she was right. And now he owed her reparation for that too. Quite apart from all the other stuff between them.

He looked down at her as her head drooped sideways against the upholstery. Several strands of hair, moonlight-pale in the shadows of the car interior, had drifted across her mouth. Still sleeping, she huffed at them. Without success. She huffed again, frowning. Very gently, Kazim brushed the hair away with a gloved finger. Her head slipped a little further.

How fragile she looked. Her eyelashes were much darker than her hair. They looked like smudges of soot against the porcelain skin. Asleep, her mouth had a sweet curve. No sign now of the abrasive independence that infuriated him.

She gave a soft sigh. Her head finally came to rest on his shoulder. Kazim held himself very still.

Natasha turned sleepily and nuzzled her head into the pillow. It was a long time since she had felt so peaceful and now she was swinging in a hammock to the scent of exotic trees and the steady pounding of the sea against the shore. I needed a holiday, she thought lazily. Now the wedding is over, I can really start enjoying it. She stretched voluptuously.

An amused voice said in her ear, 'Do you want me to carry you in?'

Even then Natasha did not quite come out of her dream.

'Mmm,' she said appreciatively.

The pillow heaved with silent laughter.

'This,' remarked Kazim to the shadows, 'is unexpected.'

He propped her up gently against the back of her seat. Natasha murmured protestingly and scrabbled to keep her warm pillow where it was. Kazim firmly detached her arm and eased himself out of the car before she could make another grab.

Natasha came to with a shock. For a moment she did not know where she was. The thunk of the driver's door closing still echoed in her head, but the darkness bewildered her. Where was the scent of spice? Where was the sea?

Then there was a gust of cool air as her own door opened and she found herself looking up into the privately amused eyes of Sheikh Kazim al Saraq. She blinked.

'Back with the world?' he asked blandly. 'How disappointing.'

Natasha shook her sleep-fuddled head. 'What—?'

'I drove you home,' he explained briefly. 'We are now outside your block.'

'Oh.' She look round blankly. Slowly the building behind him began to make sense. 'So we are.'

He opened the door. 'Come along, then. Or would you really like me to carry you, after all?'

That brought her upright at once.

'No, thank you,' she said hastily. She suppressed a yawn. 'Good night.'

But he did not take the hint. Instead he gave her one of those annoying smiles.

'I will see you to your door, at least.'

She got out—and staggered as the spring night air struck her.

'Make that bed,' he said, amused. 'You're asleep on your feet.'

He put a strong arm round her. It made her shiver. Not with tiredness.

Suddenly she was in the world of her dreams, again; dreams and fantasies and overheated imagination, where there might be crowds or emptiness, but there was always this one man. Because he belonged there. With her.

Natasha's heart began to thud like a steam hammer. All she could think was that she had been waiting for this for the whole of her life.

She did not say a word as they rode up in the silent lift together. She could almost hear the blood in her veins. In his too.

She thought: This is crazy.

She thought: I'm not ready for this.

But then, would she ever be ready? How did you prepare for a character change of this magnitude?

Half of her wanted to take his hand. Half of her wanted to run like hell.

And then the unforeseen took over again, and changed everything. She remembered the state of her bedroom!

For the last three days she had been simply stepping out of her clothes before falling into bed. She tried to remember whether you could still see the carpet and decided that you probably couldn't. The cleaning lady was not due until tomorrow. Kazim al Saraq could *not* see what a tip she slept in... Oh, why hadn't she at least hung up her clothes before she'd left this morning? Was there a chance of getting him in there without switching on the light?

And then they were at her door. Kazim took her key from her, without asking, and opened it.

At last, common sense kicked in. Let him into her flat again? Well, maybe, just this once. But let him into her bedroom? Not a chance. She must be out of her mind even to consider it.

Only Kazim was not asking her permission. He was marching her across the flat with determination...half her heart and the whole of the rest of her body was on his side...and the snooze in the car had slowed her reflexes...and...and...

The bedroom was worse than she remembered. She had still not unpacked from her last trip. The case was open on a chair, a pearly shirt falling out of it. One sleeve dangled like the arm of an abandoned nightclub singer. The carpet was strewn with books and papers as well as discarded clothes.

Nothing was really dirty. Just grubby and creased and in need of refreshing. As I am myself, thought Natasha. She grimaced and took a step away from him. Two steps. Several.

Kazim stopped dead, momentarily sidetracked. He looked round in silence.

No stranger to female bedrooms, he usually enjoyed the sensation of visiting a strange country. In his experience women enjoyed living in a froth of feminine clutter. But this was something else.

'You *sleep* here?' he said, astonished. 'How?'

Natasha retreated the rest of the way to the window. 'What do you mean?'

He shook his head, apparently dazed. 'All these things…'

That surprised her. She looked round. Well, perhaps there was rather a lot of books about. She tended to put them down where she could find a space. And maybe the joya plant on the window sill was getting out of control. As for the papers—she liked to reread a draft report in the morning just after she had woken up, when she could come to it fresh and relaxed and look at it from the client's point of view. She just had not realised how many of the discarded reports were still lying about.

She winced, but said firmly, 'Creative people are always untidy.'

Kazim looked fascinated. 'You mean it's always like this?'

She put a hand to her head. 'Please. It's too late at night to discuss my lack of housekeeping skills.'

He looked startled. 'Was that what I was doing?'

'Well, you weren't making mad, passionate love to me,' retorted Natasha unwisely.

'Ah.'

She closed her eyes. 'Why did I say that?' she moaned.

'A good question.' He sounded maddeningly *interested,* as if he'd be happy to start a debate on the subject. But not as if it mattered at all. 'Why do you think?'

She opened her eyes. She was definitely not going to make a major life change tonight. Not when he sounded like that. She told her pulses to put themselves on hold and pulled herself together.

'Tiredness,' she said crisply.

Kazim was very still. He searched her face for a long moment.

At last he said gently, 'I'm getting conflicting messages here. Which is right?'

Natasha avoided his eyes. 'I told you earlier. I'm not your girlfriend.'

There was a little silence. Then he straightened. 'You did, indeed. How could I have forgotten?'

She had not realised that she had been holding her breath until it escaped in a great sigh. Of relief, she assured herself. Of relief.

'Very well. I will go.'

But still he stood in the doorway. And she could not seem to drag her eyes away.

She said his name under her breath. For all her resolve, all the longing of those hungry dreams was in her voice. She heard it. Did he?

It shocked her, hearing it aloud. Her hands flew to her cheeks and she shut her eyes tight. 'Oh, *no!*'

When she opened her eyes, he had gone. The apartment was silent.

CHAPTER TEN

I DON'T believe it. I nearly made love with him. I wanted to. I damn nearly begged him to. I only got away by sheer chance. What is happening to me?

This fantasy has got to stop. NOW.

It was a beautiful day for a wedding. The late-spring sun shone. The breeze bounced up just enough to billow the bride's veil into a magic cloud as she walked into the old church.

The bride was wide-eyed with happiness. The groom stood tall and spoke proudly. They exchanged private smiles, full of trust, as they made their vows. The small congregation wept with luxurious sentiment. The organ cascaded music over their triumphant heads.

The chief bridesmaid juggled bouquets, order of service, and a small recalcitrant pageboy with smiling efficiency. The only time she faltered was when the pageboy was scooped away by a teenage bridesmaid and she had to follow bride and groom down the aisle, arm in arm with the best man.

Surely a woman ought to look happier to be paired, however briefly, with someone so spectacularly handsome? But she left his side as soon as she decently could. Anyone watching would have seen that she did not go near him during the reception either. Not even when the bride and groom had left and people were wandering round the garden, paradisal in the twilight with irises and early lilac.

Kazim gave the party twenty minutes to disperse. Then tracked her down.

Natasha had made herself a mug of plain coffee and got as far as the orchard. That look between Izzy and Dom—total trust, total kindness—had left her badly shaken. That and the way

Kazim, seeing it too, had tightened his hold on her hand until she'd thought her finger bones would break.

She tried hard to tell herself that weddings did that to everyone. So far she was not convinced. She prowled among the fruit trees, sipping at the comforting coffee, when suddenly a tall figure loomed out of the shadows. She shrieked and nearly dropped her mug.

'What are *you* doing here?' she said, shocked out of the carefully impersonal courtesy she had hidden behind all day.

Kazim's eyes narrowed, but he stayed polite. 'I have been looking for you. I wondered if there was anything I could do to help. Where were you?'

Natasha pushed a hand through her hair. The rose wreath had descended beyond recovery during the clearing up process. It had come to rest just above her right ear. She shook her head impatiently, but the thing was lodged.

'I was in the kitchen,' she said dryly. 'I had to pay the waiters.'

Kazim stiffened. 'I would have done that.' Still just about polite, but there was an edge to his voice.

Natasha shrugged. 'Actually, I don't think that's one of your jobs. The reception is the bride's responsibility. On this occasion, I'm the bride's infantry.'

'It is not something a woman should be asked to do,' Kazim said arctically.

Natasha looked at him in disbelief. 'Oh, come *on.*'

'Her father was here,' Kazim went on, pursuing his own line of thought. 'Why did he not pay these people?'

Natasha thought of Izzy's gentle father, struggling manfully with collar studs and a tailcoat—to say nothing of making a speech to what had turned out to be five hundred people. He had held up pretty well, considering, she thought, especially with Dom's overbearing stepmother dogging his footsteps and apologising to her smarter guests for him. Natasha had been furious and smuggled him away not long after Izzy and Dom left.

'Because he's not that sort of father,' she snapped now, bristling.

Kazim's strained courtesy finally gave way. 'Or because you did not give him the chance.'

She stopped fussing with her hair. 'What do you mean?'

'You're a control junkie. You bark out orders. You have to have your own way all the time. You never compromise. And you never listen.'

Natasha was utterly taken aback. 'All this because I paid a few waiters?'

That brought him up short. Kazim was disconcerted—and furious about it.

Natasha made a discovery. 'I think you've got a conscience about leaving me to carry all your side of the wedding arrangements.'

'I did not—'

She decided to be magnanimous. 'I forgive you.'

That made him even more furious. 'There you go, not listening again. I have nothing to have a conscience about,' he announced. 'I consider that I have treated you with outstanding forbearance. Even chivalry.'

Natasha's eyes bulged. '*Chivalry?*'

'The last time we met, if you remember,' he said deliberately, 'I left. Although you virtually invited me to stay the night.'

Natasha went scarlet to her lopsided rose wreath. 'I don't know what you're talking about,' she blustered unwisely.

'I think you do.'

'Not a clue.'

'You called me back. "Kazim", you said.'

She stared at him, hot and cold and appalled and, yet, somehow, relieved.

'I didn't think you'd heard!'

'I heard.'

She felt as if she were suffocating. 'I was too tired to know what I was saying.'

He looked smug. 'Quite. So I did not take advantage of it. That's chivalry. You could try a bit of appreciation here, Ms Control Freak.'

He was laughing at her again! It was too much.

Natasha flung her mug at him. In the half dark, her aim was poor and it crashed harmlessly against the bole of an apple tree, but it made him jump. Then she saw that she had not quite finished the coffee before she'd thrown it. The dregs had splattered his immaculate morning coat. Watching him brush at them, Natasha felt a childish rush of satisfaction.

It gave her the courage to say, 'I would have to be half asleep to let you touch me.'

Kazim gave a soft laugh. 'I can live with that.' And added, to Natasha's final outrage, 'You're very alluring when you're half asleep.'

'You—' She could not find the words. So she glared at him silently, her hands clenching and unclenching.

He did not move a muscle, just stood there smiling gently, one eyebrow raised.

And suddenly, in spite of her angry embarrassment, in spite of his wicked teasing—it was there between them. As loudly as if he had actually said it again. *It would take just one night…*

And it would. I would. Suddenly Natasha knew it, as she knew her own name. It was like stepping into a lift and finding there was nothing there. Her clenching hands stilled. She found she could not speak.

It sobered him as none of her words or flying coffee had done. He said roughly, 'Don't look like that.'

She moistened her lips. 'Like what?'

'Horrified.' His voice was light, but it was easy to see that he was not amused any more. Not a whit.

Natasha said with difficulty, 'Not horrified.'

'Then you do a good imitation of it,' he said dryly. 'What's wrong? One moment we're flirting happily. The next you look as if you've been struck from a great height.'

She shook her head, bringing her voice under her control with an effort. 'Shock,' she said with a good imitation of flippancy. 'I don't do flirting, normally.' She gave an artificial laugh. 'No time.'

His eyes narrowed and he did not smile at the attempted joke. 'Then make time.' It was brisk to the point of curtness.

Natasha was not sure she had heard right. 'What?'

He stepped closer.

Natasha fixed her eyes firmly on his silver cravat and waistcoat and began to gabble. 'Oh, dear, that coffee really did go everywhere, didn't it? I'm so sorry. I'll get a cloth...'

He stopped her by the simple expedient of taking hold of both her hands.

'Forget the coffee. Let's talk about why you don't flirt.'

She shook her head, trying to remove her hands. 'It's—just not my area of expertise.'

He held onto her. 'So I gather. I'd like to know why.'

'Who knows why anyone does anything?' she hedged.

'Ah, but I suspect you know all about your own motivations. You're the most self-aware woman I've ever met.'

She was shocked into silence.

He touched her cheek, a butterfly's wingtip of a touch, as if he was afraid she would recoil violently from anything more decided. Natasha held herself so still she could hardly breathe.

Kazim sighed. He let her hands go and stepped back. 'Walk with me?'

After a moment she nodded.

He did not touch her again, but indicated a gate at the corner of the orchard. Of course, he was Dom's friend, she thought distractedly. He must have been to Dom's house many times before. She followed him through the trees.

It was like walking in a snowstorm. Little showers of white and shell-pink blossom fell where his shoulder touched low-lying branches. In the cloud of blossom, he looked like the prince out of every fairy story she had ever read. Natasha thought: I'll never forget this moment.

Kazim led the way out of the gate into a small wooded area. The ground was a carpet of violets and primroses, studded with the star flowers of wood anemones. The evening air was sharp with the scents of leaf mould and new life. Every branch and twig was bursting into a thousand greens. Somewhere a stream gurgled.

Natasha said involuntarily, 'Oh, this is paradise.'

He smiled faintly. 'A very English paradise. Still no stars, though.'

Her bridesmaid's skirts rustled last year's leaves into little droves as she picked her way towards the river. Kazim followed watchfully. Once she turned her heel and he reached out to steady her instinctively. But she had already righted herself. His hand fell to his side.

He said, 'Were you always this independent?'

Ah, thought Natasha. Time for truth. Oh, well, why not?

'No,' she said baldly. 'I started off thinking other people meant their promises.'

He scanned her face gravely. 'A man let you down?' He sounded surprised.

'It's not as simple as that—'

'It wouldn't be,' he agreed. 'Want to tell me what happened? In the jungle, I think.'

Natasha went stone cold. '*What?*'

'So I'm right.'

She swung furiously round on him. Leaves flew with the violence of the movement. 'You've been spying on me. You set one of your thugs in sunglasses to dig around in my past. Didn't you?'

'No.' He looked sad. 'No. I wouldn't do that.'

'I don't believe you,' she spat.

'Think about it. When we had dinner, I asked you where your spiritual home was. The way you reacted to the word ''jungle'' worried me.'

Frustrated, Natasha stared at him, hot-eyed. He returned her look calmly.

'Going to tell me about it?' he prompted.

She shut her eyes. She had never told anyone. Not about the bad stuff. 'It's all behind me,' she said curtly.

'If that's true, then you won't care whether you tell me or not,' said that quiet voice with relentless reason.

She opened her eyes. Suddenly she was angry, more than angry, furious.

'Okay,' she said tensely. 'If you have to know. After uni I went travelling. Ended in the jungle, as you guessed.'

'With a man?'

She was curt. 'Yes. I thought we were—together, partners. Two against the world, sort of thing. I trusted him.' She swallowed.

She did not know how desolate she sounded.

Kazim said nothing. A little muscle began to work in his cheek.

She gave herself a mental shake. 'Well, he got involved with a group I didn't like. In the end they said they were going to hold us for ransom. He did a deal and got away. Without me. I realised then—you can't expect anyone else to look after you.'

He said on a note of discovery, 'You were in love with him.'

Her jaw was so tight, he could see the tremor. 'I got over it.'

His eyes searched her face. 'Did they hurt you?'

She gave a grim laugh. 'I learned some valuable lessons about people, geography and evasive tactics. And I got out. The whole thing even came in useful when I was on a tour bus that got ambushed, years later.'

His jaw was like concrete, but at this he looked up. 'That's when you met Izzy?'

'That's right. I got us out of the jungle. *I* did. Because I didn't count on anyone but me,' she said fiercely.

Kazim was very pale. 'Not even Izzy?'

Natasha shrugged. 'Izzy's great. But if she hadn't been there, I'd still have got out. Maybe not all the others would have come too. But I'd have done it.'

'I believe you,' he said suddenly. 'But does that mean you have to give up trusting?'

'Yes,' she said baldly.

He thought about that for a few seconds. Then he nodded. 'Okay, I see that. But do you have to stop having fun as well?'

That disconcerted her. 'I have fun.'

'Do you? Workaholic days and empty nights don't sound like a lot of fun to me.'

It was a body blow. Natasha did not even try to answer.

His voice softened. 'Why don't you give yourself a chance?'

'What sort of chance?' Her voice sounded stifled, even to her own ears. She could not bear to look at him.

'Take off for a while. Leave your assistant to run the business. Put in some practice on your flirting technique.'

She was so startled she forgot she was not going to look at him. Her eyes flew to his face—and found that his were oddly intent. And he had the longest eyelashes she had ever seen on a man. How would they feel against her skin if…?

'I don't follow,' said Natasha, distracted.

'I'm offering you the chance of some high-class tuition,' said Kazim, amused and much, much more. 'Come away with me. You said yourself you need a holiday.'

Her eyes widened. 'With you?'

The corners of his eyes crinkled, though his mouth stayed prim.

'I can do you waving palms, balmy breezes and warm sea,' he offered. 'And some great stars. What do you say to a few days of total peace?'

'With *you*?'

The crinkles disappeared. Suddenly he wasn't laughing any more.

Kazim said deliberately, 'You can see as much or as little of me as you want. I told you. Chivalry.'

Natasha was unbearably tempted. If he had taken her in his arms… If he had just touched her hand again… If he had said just one word of affection…

Oh, boy. Affection. Who was she fooling? What she meant was love, wasn't it?

Suddenly Natasha felt sick. She realised that for one word of love she would have gone with him anywhere.

But this was not love. This was Kazim attempting to rescue a terminal workaholic, with a small experiment in superflirting on the side. He was too sophisticated for anything as simple as love.

And so am I, thought Natasha. And so am I.

For the first time in years, she regretted that brittle sophistication she had cultivated so carefully. Oh, sure, it meant she could hold her own in every social and professional situation. But it didn't do much for honesty and kindness.

Slowly, she shook her head, turning away so he should not see the suspicious moisture in her eyes.

'Not my scene.' It was quick, hard-sounding.

He made an instinctive move towards her, quickly curbed. She refused to see it.

'I must go. Time I was on my way back to London.' She took off for the gate into the orchard at a tearing rate. 'Sorry,' she flung over her shoulder as she went. She did not care whether it sounded as unconvincing to him as it did to her. All she wanted to do was get away—and get away now.

She did not look back, just in case he tried to persuade her. It would not take much to change her mind.

And that, thought Natasha, would change her whole life.

Kazim followed her more slowly. He was furious with himself.

What had got into him? He had been so clear of his strategy— charm her a little, make her laugh, make her feel safe. Then suggest, ever so subtly, that she should see his country. That it would be fun, even educational.

Instead, he had looked down at that tremulous mouth, trying so hard to pretend that she was indifferent, and forgotten every vestige of his careful plan. Oh, really great going, for a professional negotiator! And then he'd committed the cardinal sin— backed her into a corner. He had left her nowhere to go and she'd ended up baring her guarded soul to him!

Kazim groaned aloud. Would she ever forget that self-betrayal? No. Would she ever forgive him? No, again.

And, to crown it all, he'd completely lost the plot and offered her a crash course on flirting! He could not have done worse if he had been a crass teenager—or the cold-hearted womaniser she clearly thought he was.

'Very smooth, Kazim,' he muttered.

He ought to get after her fast and do whatever he could to put it right.

Yet, even as he increased his pace the wiser, more responsible bit of his brain was saying, 'Give her a break. This is a woman who has had more than her fair share of political agitators already. And now you want to pull her into the terrorist soup with you?'

He stopped dead.

'I never give up,' said the Emir's grandson.

'But it wouldn't be fair to her,' said the international seeker after truth and justice.

'I don't believe I've seen the last of those furry feet,' said Kazim the irrepressible optimist.

'She won't forgive you for that either,' said the pessimist.

That was when his cell phone rang.

Irritated, he flicked the screen open. It was Tom. If it had been anyone but his Head of Security, he would have left the call. But Tom would not call unless it was urgent.

'What is it, Tom?'

And it was bad news. The picture of Kazim and Natasha outside the restaurant had surfaced at last. Worse—one of the security agencies had leaked it days ago. Several of the groups opposed to Kazim's peace initiative had already shown interest.

Kazim was coldly, violently furious. 'You mean some secret serviceman on the make has turned Natasha Lambert into bait to get the insurgents out into the open.'

Tom did not answer that directly. 'The sooner you get her out of there, the better, Kazim.' There was no mistaking the urgency in his voice.

Kazim closed his eyes briefly. And he had just done a fabulous job of giving the woman every reason to reject going anywhere with him.

He considered rapidly. No matter which way he looked at it, he kept coming back to the same solution. Natasha would never forgive him, of course. But at least it would keep her safe, while the security services did their work.

'There's only one place I am certain I can protect her,' he said heavily. 'Get the jet up to a local airfield and I'll fly out tonight.'

'You're taking her to your grandfather's?'

Kazim said slowly, 'No, I'm taking her to the desert. Hell, that's why my grandfather gave me the Sultana's Palace in the first place. Get Martin to call ahead and have them prepare some rooms.'

You could see the stars from the roof of the little palace; see the stars and breathe in the spice winds off the Indian Ocean. He could take her on the roof and show her the stars she could never find in London. And maybe, when it was all over, she would at least have one good memory of him.

Maybe.

'Oh, and Tom—'

'Yes?'

'Better organise some clothes for her too.'

'The—er—usual?' asked Tom discreetly. He had heard about Kazim's romantic encounters, though Kazim was always meticulous in keeping his staff out of his private arrangements. This was the first time he had ever asked Tom or anyone else to help organise a liaison.

Kazim flinched. 'Clothes for the climate, Tom, not the boudoir.'

It was, he found, almost shamefully easy to lure Natasha to the airport. He sent one of the waiters to find her with a message that Izzy had forgotten an essential bag. Please would Tash bring it along to the airport at once? He even gave the man a case to take to her with the message. He stood hidden under tumbling cherry blossoms to watch her get into the back of the car and be driven off. She was still wearing the bridesmaid's dress, but she tore off the ruined wreath and lobbed it into the bushes before she got into the car.

As her car disappeared down the drive he picked up the wreath and smoothed its petals as gently as he had touched her face that night she'd fallen asleep on his shoulder. She would never fall asleep on his shoulder again, he thought. He would be lucky if she would even speak to him.

He straightened. Still, she would be alive. Hating him, but alive. It was something.

He set the rest of his arrangements in motion.

*   *   *

Natasha was so tired, she dozed in the back of the car as it sped down unfamiliar lanes. It was only when it pulled into a slip road and began to slow down that she sat up and began to take notice.

'Where are we?'

But she did not need to ask. The answer was plain to see, with all the small planes parked along the edge of the field.

'There's been a mistake—' she began.

But the car swept past the airfield buildings and the parked planes and went to the very edge of the tarmac, where an executive jet was parked. It was bigger than anything else on the field and in the semi-dark she could make out that there was a pilot in uniform and braid standing beside it. But it did not take the fancy braid to tell her whose plane this was.

She bundled her taffeta skirts round her and shot out of the limo.

'Where is he?' she said grimly.

Kazim appeared at the top of the steps. 'Good evening, Natasha.'

Her first feeling was one of ridiculous joy. The second, terror that he would find it out.

'What are you doing here? And how did you get here before me?'

'Taking you away from all this. And a helicopter.'

Natasha resisted a low desire to allow herself to be swept off her feet and carried off to his palm trees and balmy breezes. 'No, you're not taking me away. I thought I made myself clear.'

'You did,' he agreed. He ran lightly down the companionway. 'Would you like me to carry you aboard? In lieu of throwing you across my saddle, I mean.'

In spite of herself, Natasha laughed. 'Dinosaur,' she said softly.

'Guilty,' he agreed.

'You're quite mad,' sighed Natasha, deeply pleased. 'I haven't even got my passport.'

'You are my guest,' said Kazim superbly. 'In my country that is passport enough.'

He urged her up the steps into the plane and led her into the luxurious interior. Natasha followed him—out of curiosity, she assured herself—but she still shook her head. 'But without a passport, they'll never let me back home again.'

'My people have it in hand.' Kazim ushered her into a cream leather seat as deeply cushioned as any state-of-the-art armchair. He sat down opposite her, his eyes dancing. 'How does it feel, not being in control for once?'

A shadow crossed her face. 'It's not exactly a new experience,' she said sharply.

He stilled, the amusement dying out of his face as he remembered her experiences in the jungle. 'Of course. I'm sorry. I—forgot.'

Natasha looked away, annoyed with herself. 'It's in the past.'

'If only that were true,' murmured Kazim involuntarily.

But, looking out of the porthole, she saw a man hurrying towards the plane. As he came into the lights of the stationary plane, she saw more gold braid. 'Who is this?' she said sharply.

Kazim looked out. 'The copilot,' he said indifferently. 'The paperwork must be finished.'

'Ah.' Natasha wrapped her arms round herself.

He was leaving. Whether she went too or not, he was leaving tonight. After that, there was no reason why they should ever meet again. They had nothing in common. They were hardly ever in the same country. No, they would never meet again. Unless she went with him after all…

It was nonsense, of course. No self-respecting twenty-first-century woman would let herself be carried off in this high-handed fashion. Of course she wouldn't. And Natasha had more reason than most women to resist testosterone-driven commands.

And yet—

Kazim sat back in the luxurious seat, frowning. His eyes were hooded and he seemed very far away, all of a sudden. Far away and not at all happy, thought Natasha.

Her heart twisted. She put out a hand. 'Kazim—'

It brought him out of his reverie. His eyes lifted and he looked at her almost ruefully. 'Okay. You win.'

Natasha stared. It was the last thing she expected. 'What?'

'If you're absolutely determined not to sample the palm trees, now is the time to get off the plane.'

His words were determinedly frivolous. So why was she certain to her bones that there was something deadly serious here? She sat up straight and met his eyes.

'You really want me to come with you?' she said quietly.

A muscle moved convulsively in his jaw. But all he said was, 'It's the only thing I want.'

It looked honest. And yet—

Natasha was in a muddle and she knew it. Repressed anger rippled under the words like a rip tide. Or did they? What did he have to be angry about? And what did he mean, *the only thing he wanted?*

She scanned his face. But the handsome, clever features told her nothing.

She stood up.

Suddenly, shockingly, his face was stripped. He looked appalled. Just for a moment, of course. Then the courteous mask was in place again and he was on his feet too. But there was no mistaking his reaction when he thought she would leave him.

'I must be mad,' said Natasha.

And sat down again.

Kazim looked as if he didn't believe it. 'You'll come with me?' He did not attempt to touch her. But his eyes burned.

Natasha found she could not meet that intensity. She looked away. To ease the charged atmosphere, she said with an attempt at lightness, 'Looks like it.'

He closed his eyes briefly, as if he could not believe it; as if he had not dared to let himself hope.

That had to be her own wish fulfilment, Natasha told herself bracingly. Didn't it?

She rubbed her arms and made a brave attempt at lightening the charged atmosphere. 'As long as I can borrow a change of clothes. I'm not galloping around the desert in bridesmaid's taffeta.'

'Of course.' His voice was strained. 'Maryam will find you something for the journey.' He raised a hand and a uniformed flight attendant appeared from behind a curtain. He did not look at her. 'A robe for madam.'

The attendant disappeared silently.

Kazim still did not take his eyes off Natasha. 'What changed your mind?'

She shifted her shoulders. 'Oh, I don't know.' The contrived lightness was becoming a strain. 'Maybe because you'd gone to such pains to get me here. I suppose I'm intrigued.'

Kazim blinked. It was like having a searchlight turned off. Natasha could have sighed with relief. Or disappointment. She was not sure which.

'Intrigued!' He sounded almost affronted.

'Great marketing,' she told him flippantly.

'That was not my intention—' he began grimly. But was interrupted.

It was one of the pilots, apologetic but determined. Behind him was the man she had last seen at Serenata Place looking at her shoe as if it were a home-made bomb. Natasha flinched at the memory.

Kazim stalked over to them. He talked briefly, quietly, to the pilot, who nodded and went off to the cockpit. Almost at once the plane began to hum as electronic systems came online.

He brought the other man back to Natasha.

'This is my security adviser, Tom Soltano. Ms Lambert has decided to come to Saraq for a visit, Tom.'

The man nodded pleasantly. 'Good to have you with us, Ms Lambert. Kazim, there are a couple of reports you should look at as soon as you can.'

Kazim bowed to her apologetically. 'I'm afraid I have to work now. Are you warm enough? You can go to bed once we've taken off. But Maryam will bring you that wrap now. And you must have some of our Arabic coffee.'

It set the tone for the whole flight. Kazim and his security adviser sat at a small low table and talked in low, urgent voices or consulted a thin silver laptop that was clearly state-of-the-art.

It was as if Kazim felt he did not need to try any more. She had agreed to come. End of project.

'Good marketing. Rotten after sales,' muttered Natasha. But not to Kazim.

Meanwhile the smiling attendant made sure that Natasha had everything she wanted. She brought her coffee and fruit and, eventually, showed her to a sleeping cubicle that was as compact as it was private.

Natasha half expected Kazim to join her, if not at once, then as soon as he had finished his business. But it was kindly Maryam who helped her off with the light wool robe and the hopelessly creased bridesmaid's dress and tucked her up under a dreamily luxurious duvet. Natasha tried to keep her eyes open, for surely he would come soon. But there was still a low buzz of conversation from the other part of the cabin and, somehow, she could not seem to keep her eyes open.

She slept fitfully. Every time she came awake the thrum of the engines gave her a shock. But then she remembered that Kazim was on the plane somewhere and went quietly back to sleep. He might have terrible after-sales strategy, she thought with a muzzy grin, but they had unfinished business. Kazim would not leave her until they brought it to a conclusion, one way or another. She knew that, as surely as she knew herself.

It was dark when they arrived in Saraq. Maryam woke Natasha before landing, but she was still yawning when she made her way down the steps onto a deserted airfield, with only the smallest bungalow of an airport building. A cold wind whipped at the skirts of her robe. She missed her footing on the bottom step and found a strong arm round her.

'You're still half asleep,' said Kazim, helping her down the last step.

Natasha bristled. 'Well, I've got a lot of sleep to catch up on,' she retorted. 'I've been doing the best man's job as well as the bridesmaid's, if you remember.'

He was dry. 'If you want to make me feel terrible, you're succeeding.'

'Good.'

The wind gusted again and she staggered. His arm tightened, not quite as it had in the church. Even so, Natasha's blood began to pound uncomfortably.

To cover it up, she said brightly, 'Hey, I was promised palm trees and sun. This feels more like Siberia.'

'The desert is very cold at night. Wait till noon. You'll get sun so strong it makes your eyes water. Trust me.'

But she was shivering steadily now. The soft cashmere robe was just not adequate to keep out the pre-dawn gusts.

Kazim clicked his tongue impatiently and flicked an imperious finger. At once a big off-road vehicle tore across the tarmac and slewed to a halt beside them. The driver leaped out and offered the keys respectfully. But Kazim shook his head. Instead, he opened the door to the back seat and more or less lifted her into it.

It was blessedly warm. Natasha began to feel more human. She even smiled at him.

But he did not smile back. And he did not get in beside her.

'Go with Ali. There is something I have to do. Then I'll join you. There's a room prepared for you.' He closed the door on her. 'Get her to the Sultana's Palace,' he told the driver curtly.

He raised a hand as the car pulled away. In fact he stood watching her all the way across the airport. Natasha slewed round in her seat to see. Beside him, Tom was trying to attract his attention but Kazim did not even know he was there. He was staring after her departing vehicle as if she were setting off for the moon.

It was only as the car pulled out onto a metalled track that Natasha thought suddenly: He looks as if he never expects to see me again.

CHAPTER ELEVEN

'THEY were waiting for Natasha at her apartment,' Tom said briefly. He thrust a paper at Kazim. 'The London police arrested them. But—'

Kazim assimilated the contents rapidly and saw a name he recognised. His head came up, startled. 'That man is here?'

'Well, in Saraq,' agreed Tom.

'You can drive across Saraq in two days,' pointed out Kazim. 'With a helicopter, they could be here before breakfast. Has he got a helicopter?'

Tom nodded, slowly.

Kazim thought. 'Okay. Let's talk about options.'

That dash across the pre-dawn desert was the worst journey of Natasha's life; worse even than those heart-stopping trudges through the jungle. The shadows were formless. The headlights picked out nothing but dunes and emptiness. And all she could think of was Kazim standing as if he would never move again, looking after her car as if it was for the last time. It was like the worst sort of nightmare.

She barely took in the desert palace, with its perimeter wall and mediaeval tower, overlooking a sickle-shaped bay. All she wanted was to see Kazim again and banish the nightmare.

'For you,' said a smiling woman, taking her to a room full of carved screens and tasselled sofas, strewn with jewel-coloured cushions. She flung open an exquisitely wrought door, to reveal a well-stocked walk-in closet, and another to show an incongruous fridge.

Beyond the delicate shutters, there was the soft hush of the ocean. Natasha ignored it, the clothes and the contents of the fridge alike. She twisted her hands.

'Thank you. But Kazim?'

The woman beamed. 'His Excellency's compliments. He will join you when you have rested.'

Natasha had to be content with that.

But he was not there when the dawn came up, turning the sand beyond her window first to silver, then to gold. Natasha got up from a restless sleep and pulled on the first garments her hand fell on. They turned out to be soft silky trousers and a sleeveless shirt—simple enough, but the designer labels told their own story. And their smell was familiar.

Amertage, thought Natasha, her heart lurching. So which of Kazim's girlfriends had worn these delicate things before her? She winced, then told herself firmly that it didn't matter.

'We're both adults. We're both bound to have a history.' They would laugh about it once he joined her.

Only he did not join her. He was not there when a smiling woman brought her fruit and headily aromatic tea onto the little battlemented terrace that overlooked the bay outside her room. He was still not there when the sun blazed overhead at midday and all the shadows turned as thin as a needle, then disappeared, and the woman brought her a lemon drink, sweet and sharp.

'His Excellency?' Natasha said.

The woman still smiled. 'He will come.'

Natasha smiled back, but it was an effort. She could not forget that look on his face as she'd been driven away. As if he thought he would never see her again.

Restlessly, she began to prowl through quiet rooms.

Kazim had called it a palace, but the place was not large. If anything, it felt like a guard tower, which someone had adapted into an exquisitely comfortable retreat. The walls were simple stone, but the rooms were filled with miraculously carved doors and screens; curved and scalloped arches; columns like twists of barley sugar; and, everywhere, carpets like jewels, alive with ruby and coral, lapis lazuli and turquoise.

With Kazim beside her, it would have been a fairy tale. With this awful fear round her heart, it was a horror.

Natasha took hold of herself. 'Am I a woman or a mouse? If you're scared there's only one thing to do. Turn and face it.'

She quartered the palace in a businesslike search for someone or something she could face. In the end she went down a tiny stone corridor that smelled of coffee and fresh-baked bread and found herself in a space-age office. The security adviser—the one who sported the assassin's shades—was standing by a desk, peering as messages flashed up on a computer screen.

Natasha gathered herself together, squared her shoulders and marched in.

'What's going on?' she demanded.

He spun round, startled. 'Ms Lambert! I didn't hear you.'

'Where is Kazim?' She was very calm. And quite implacable. 'I think it's time you told me, don't you?'

She saw him assess her, note the steady eyes and determined chin, and bow to the inevitable. She hid her amusement. But when he started to speak, all desire to laugh fled. She listened to him in gathering disbelief.

In the end, she repeated the only thing that she could get hold of. 'Kazim is afraid that he's put me in danger, just by bringing me here?'

Tom looked momentarily astonished. 'Hell, no. We brought you here to get you *out* of danger.'

We brought you here? Natasha suddenly felt very cold.

Tom did not notice. 'Kazim didn't like it,' he assured her earnestly. 'We're the good guys here. We don't go round kidnapping people.'

Her lips felt anaesthetised. 'Of course not,' she managed.

'But we couldn't think of anything to do. There was a photograph of you and Kazim together, you see. Normally he's so careful to keep his—er—lady friends out of the spotlight.'

Natasha winced. Tom did not notice.

'The problem is that it put you in the frame as someone who Kazim—' He hesitated.

'Had once taken to a public restaurant?' flashed Natasha. 'Big deal!'

Tom was even more concerned. 'I know it sounds crazy. But

the word has got round that you're important to him.' He laughed heartily.

Natasha laughed too. To her great relief he did not seem to notice how hollow it was.

'That photo has been made to look all sorts of things that it wasn't. We suspect that security services are doing it deliberately, using you to bait a trap. Anyway, the damage is done now. So Kazim and I talked it over and decided that we could protect you better here.'

Natasha felt as if all her limbs had turned to ice. 'How inventive of them,' she said mechanically.

Tom flashed her a relieved smile. Had he expected her to scream and faint? Somewhere, at the edge of the ice plain that her heart had become, that really irritated her.

'Kazim felt he'd got you into it. So it was up to us to get you out.'

I pay my debts. Of course he did. How could she have thought anything else? Oh, he was a charmer, but he had never given any sign that he wanted to make love to her. Hell, he'd even walked away, that night in her flat. He called it chivalry, but Natasha thought she knew better now. Simple indifference.

Yet what about him standing there at the desert airport, staring after her as if the light were going out of his life?

It was all in her head. It had to be. His assistant in the intimidating sunglasses knew the truth. He had no reason to lie. It was all down to international skulduggery and a man who paid his dues.

What a fool I've been.

Natasha pulled herself together. 'Very chivalrous,' she said with bite.

Tom was oblivious of undercurrents. He took that at face value. 'Very hot on his obligations,' he said with a grin. 'No task too big; no detail too small.'

She smiled so widely, it felt as if her mouth would crack. 'How true. After all, he even took care of a small detail like me, didn't he?'

Even Tom picked up on that one. He began to look alarmed. 'I never meant—'

Natasha groped for her own sunglasses, whipped them on and pushed them up her nose with fingers that were almost steady. She smiled brightly. 'Don't worry. It's always best to know the facts.'

'Yes, but—'

She said briskly, 'Thank you for explaining. Let me know when I can go. You are collecting my passport, I trust? Kazim said he would take care of it.'

Tom was uncomfortable. 'I'll look into it.'

'Thank you.' God, she was good at this. She sounded as crisp and unmoved as if he were a client. 'Meanwhile, I'm sure I saw sun loungers on the terrace. Time for some serious basking, I think.'

'It's really not wise to lie outside when the sun is high. Kazim would tell you—'

'But Kazim isn't here,' pointed out Natasha, her bright courtesy strained to snapping point. 'So I get to do exactly what I want. Right?'

Tom gave up.

To her fury, Natasha found he was right about the sun. In the end, she took refuge in the cool of her bedroom and sat looking out over her terrace to stone battlements and the sea beyond.

It was like being in a dream where she was the last person left alive. The palace was silent, though somewhere she knew that people were working. The shore was a great stretch of golden powder, without a footprint to mar its smoothness. No wind. No shadows. Not even a bird in the hot, still sky. It was as if the whole world were holding its breath, waiting for something to happen.

'Waiting for me to break down and scream,' Natasha told herself with bitter humour.

Or cry, maybe.

Well, they were in for a disappointment, there. She did not cry and she could handle anything; even the news that Kazim thought of her as an involuntarily acquired responsibility. Though it stung. No, more than that. It hurt; really hurt. And when she was back home, with a job to do and meetings to go to, she would *perhaps* let herself think about that.

But just now all she was going to do was empty her mind of everything except the need to stay very, very calm. And get home as soon as possible.

'What I need is a strategy,' Natasha told the ocean, dry-eyed and determined.

And Kazim?

'Oh, I don't need any strategy to deal with him.' The self-mockery was harsh. 'I may never see him again, anyway. And if I do, I shall just tell him that nobody is responsible for me. Nobody. So he can just give me my passport and cross me off the list of things he has to deal with. He can just forget me. That's what I'll tell him. If we ever meet again.'

So she was utterly unprepared for the swift step on the stone stair. When a figure in swirling white robes arrived on her terrace, she just gaped.

'You're here,' said Kazim in a quick, hard voice she had never heard from him before.

He took off the sunglasses he was wearing and rubbed his eyes as if he could not quite see properly.

Natasha stood up slowly and went out into the air. The sun beat at her. She could feel it on every inch of skin, just as she could feel his eyes, passing through the designer cotton as if it didn't exist.

She swallowed deafeningly. All the things she had been going to say to him went clean out of her head. All she could think was: He is here; he is *here.*

He said harshly, 'Are you all right?'

She nodded.

Kazim drew a huge breath as if it hurt him. 'Thank God.' His shoulders slumped and she saw how tense he must have been.

'What is it?' she said in quick concern.

'I was afraid—' He broke off, scanning her face. 'You really are all right? Not hurt? Scared?'

Suddenly Natasha remembered all the things she had been rehearsing to say to him.

'Now you listen to me,' she said with heat. 'You're not my keeper. Whatever you may have talked yourself into, I am an independent woman and I can take care of myself.'

He pushed his hand through his hair. 'In normal circumstances, of course—'

She interrupted. 'In *all* circumstances.'

He did not say anything.

She switched on one of her bright, professional smiles. 'So, you see, if you were feeling responsible for me, you can stop right now. I absolve you. You're off the hook. Give me my passport and I'll be on the next flight home. And you never have to think of me again.'

He stared at her for a long, long moment. Natasha held his eyes, unflinching, her chin high. Then he gave a laugh that was more than half a groan. And hauled her into his arms so roughly that she lost her balance.

Kazim did not kiss her, just held her against him, as if he could not believe she was there. She felt his face turning and turning against her hair. Face pressed in the folds of his soft robe, she smelled Amertage again, only now it was mixed with his warm skin, the sun-warmed cloth, and faint hint of diesel fuel.

He was murmuring into her hair. She was not sure that he meant her to hear. His broken words did not make sense. Or they made all the sense in the world.

Natasha forgot that she was going to tell him to forget her. She levered herself out of the folds of his robe far enough to breathe and put up her hands to cradle his stooped head.

'Hush,' she found herself saying. 'Hush. I'm here. I'm fine. Stop worrying.'

His arms tightened until she thought her ribs would crack. She must have protested somehow, for he relaxed his grip almost at once.

He raised his head and laughed shakily. 'I didn't realise how afraid I was…'

Natasha hardly recognised his face. There were deep indentations from mouth to nose and his eyes were bloodshot with
weariness. More than weariness. She took his hand and led him
out of the pitiless sun into the cool haven of her room.

'I think you'd better tell me,' she said gently.

He stopped on the threshold. 'Are you sure? I promised you
your privacy. Chivalry stays outside the bedroom door,' he said,
mocking himself.

'I'm sure,' said Natasha steadily. And when he still hesitated,
added teasingly, 'I trust you.'

And found, to her astonishment, that it was true.

Kazim gave a great sigh and came inside among the carvings
and the grateful shade. Natasha waved him towards a tasselled
divan while she brought him iced water from the fridge. He
drank deeply, then leaned back among the cushions, catching
her to him and taking her with him, as if he could not bear to
leave hold of her.

Natasha the spiky, the independent, the combative, let her
body fall with his as if she had been curling up against his heart
all her adult life.

'Tell me,' she said again softly.

He stroked her hair with his chin. 'How much do you know
about my life?'

Natasha thought of her exchange with his security adviser and
winced. 'More than I did twenty-four hours ago,' she said
grimly. But she stayed in his arms. 'What's-his-name—Tom—
told me you thought I'd got involved somehow.'

His ribcage lifted. She felt his gust of anger under her cheek.

'That was unforgivable. I should have been more careful.'

'Should you?'

'Of course. I'm an adult. I should have remembered what was
necessary. That what I wanted didn't matter.'

He was playing with her hair, winding a tendril round his
finger and releasing it, winding and releasing. She felt the idle
play of his hand against her exposed neck and nearly melted
with longing.

Natasha spread her hand over the white robe that covered his chest. She watched her fingernails absorbedly, phrasing her question with infinite care.

'Does that mean you want me?'

The caressing hand stopped as if she had stuck a needle in him.

Natasha levered herself away from him and turned on the divan to look into his face.

His expression was tense, guarded, unreadable. He might be about to declare undying love, or he might be astonished that she took a passing attraction so seriously. There was no way of telling what he thought. Or what he felt. If he felt anything at all, and it wasn't all in her head.

Natasha swallowed. She almost left the subject there. Almost.

But this was her whole life. She knew that now. She summoned up all her courage and met his eyes.

'Well?' It was a challenge.

Kazim closed his eyes briefly. 'Oh, God, yes, I want you. More than that.' He sounded exhausted. And his arm fell.

Natasha could not believe it. Even though he was no longer holding her, all the tension in her bones turned to air and sunlight. It flowed out of her, filling the room with joy.

'Well, then—'

He opened his eyes. His voice was low. 'Natasha, what I do— it has to be done and there isn't anyone else. Oh, there are organisations and teams and projects. But in the end people want to negotiate with a person they trust.'

Natasha's glorious sunshine dimmed a bit.

'And that has to be you?'

'That's the way it seems to have turned out. It has to be someone independent. Someone who isn't a politician. Someone who doesn't draw a salary.' He gave a faint smile. 'Not a lot of people qualify.'

The golden light was suddenly not golden any more. She said in a small voice, 'But do you have to let it eat up your whole life?'

He said simply, 'I shall always be on call. And I will always be a target.'

It was like a body blow. The light flickered and went out. Natasha picked up a cushion and hugged it to her.

There was a long silence. He did not touch her again. Eventually he stood up and went to the open French window onto the terrace. She stayed on the divan, watching him. His robes stirred softly in the breeze from the sea.

At last he said, 'I put all thought of a normal life out of my mind years ago.'

She breathed very slowly and carefully, in case the thickness in her throat showed in her voice. 'I can relate to that.'

He gave a ghost of a smile. It did not touch his eyes. 'Something we have in common. Only in your case it's because a man left you on your own to sink or swim in the jungle all those years ago.'

Her throat was now so full that she could not speak. She nodded jerkily.

'In exactly the same way as I would probably let you down.'

Natasha pressed her lips together to stop them trembling. Please don't let me sniff, she prayed.

'Like now. I walked you onto a London pavement into the lens of a paparazzo—and, bang, there you are on the front line. Because of me. Just like your boyfriend.'

'No!' she said in a strangled voice.

He swept round then, and looked at her sombrely.

'Ironic, isn't it? The only important thing I do is the one thing that gives you the horrors.'

Natasha pulled herself together. She did sniff—she had no choice—but it was a controlled and quiet sniff. She stopped cuddling the cushion like a teddy-bear substitute, put it carefully back on the divan and stood up.

'You are not in the least like my first boyfriend,' she said clearly.

There were stark indentations beside his mouth. 'If only that were true.'

'It *is* true. What sort of idiot do you think I am? I don't fall for an irresponsible jackass twice.'

He stared, arrested.

Natasha crossed the room with impatient steps. 'You're high-handed and dictatorial. A total dinosaur,' she reminded him. 'But not irresponsible. Look how you got me here because you thought you were responsible for me.'

'I *am* responsible. I put you in danger.'

'And you dealt with it. In an extremely overbearing way, if I may say so. Not too far from a kidnap. But you dealt with it.' She paused, struck. 'As a matter of interest, how *did* you deal with it?'

This time the smile reached his eyes. 'I'm afraid you will find it completely Jurassic. I've agreed to meet the leader. Just the two of us alone.'

'What? You mean you get me out of danger by walking into it yourself?'

He shrugged.

'That's not Jurassic. That's mediaeval,' said Natasha furiously.

His lips twitched. 'You could be right. Traditional, anyway.'

She found her eyes were full of tears and dashed them away impatiently. He made a move towards her, but stopped when she glared.

'It's *temper*,' she told him dangerously.

'Of course it is,' he soothed.

'I never cry.'

'I'm sure you don't.'

He produced a snowy handkerchief from a pocket in his robe. Natasha snatched it and blew her nose loudly. She blotted the skin below her eyes carefully and looked at him with acute dislike.

'Okay. Tell me about this hand-to-hand duel, then.'

He laughed aloud at that, but very gently. His eyes were so warm she almost didn't recognise him.

'Not exactly a duel. Call it a negotiation.'

'An armed negotiation?'

'Details,' he said, waving a lordly hand.

Natasha could have hit him. 'When and where?' she said crisply.

His eyes caressed her. 'Such demand for precision. I see why you are a successful businesswoman.'

'And I see why you're successful at what you do too. Never give a straight answer if you can get away without. Well, not with me, you won't, buster,' she said grimly. 'When and where?'

To her surprise he gave in. His little smile was wholly appreciative. 'Dawn tomorrow.' He nodded towards the French window. 'Out there.'

Natasha couldn't believe it. 'Out there? The sea? What on earth—? Lilos at fifty paces? Get real.'

He laughed aloud at that. 'You are a constant delight. I always think you can't surprise me any more—and then you do. No, not the sea, my darling. The desert.'

'The desert?'

His darling? His *darling?*

But Kazim did not even seem to notice what he had called her.

'I told you it was traditional,' he said with a hint of smugness. 'It's a desert parley. The full ceremony.'

But he had still called her his darling! Even if he chose to ignore it, she hadn't made a mistake about that. 'I don't understand,' said Natasha, trying to concentrate. His *darling.*

'If I had known you were interested, I would have taken you through our history and traditions with pleasure,' he teased.

Natasha narrowed her eyes at him. 'You still can. There's always tomorrow.'

The laughter leaked out of him. Slowly he shook his head and turned away. He went back onto the terrace and looked out to sea.

The breeze was stronger now. Following him, Natasha saw that the sky was darkening at a tremendous rate. Over the murmuring ocean, a sickle of moon had already appeared above the horizon.

She went and stood beside him, looking out to sea too, not quite touching him.

'All right. Not tomorrow. The day after, then.'

He stood like a rock. 'The day after you will be on your way home. Tom tells me that you have already been worrying about your passport. I promise you, it will arrive tomorrow. Then you can go back to London.'

There was something jagged and painful in her throat. 'And you? Where will you go?'

Kazim hesitated. 'Wherever I'm needed.'

'As long as I'm not there,' said Natasha, looking up at him on a flash of bitterness. 'Isn't that what you mean?'

He did not answer.

She turned on him then, trying desperately to stay logical. 'Tell me honestly. How much danger are you in tomorrow?'

Kazim did not answer at once. Natasha waited, implacable.

In the end he said carefully, 'No more danger than usual. No more than I'm used to.'

'That's no answer.'

He put his hands on her shoulders then, and turned her towards him. 'Yes, it is. Don't you understand? My life is one long desert parley of one sort or another.' He drew a deep breath. 'I'm a bad risk, Natasha.'

She stared.

The sun had almost gone. It was cold, but Natasha refused to shiver. Kazim's robe was billowing, whipping round her like an embrace.

He said, 'If we were different people... If we lived in a different world... But we don't.'

She scanned his face in the gathering darkness. Stars had appeared with startling suddenness, like a dust storm of diamonds against a black velvet sky. In the shadows, his arrogant profile was uncompromising.

But he had called her his darling. She said softly, 'You want me. You said so.'

'I also said that I'm a bad risk,' he reminded her.

Natasha realised she was fighting for her life here. 'And if it's a risk I want to take?'

He was very still. 'You don't know what it would mean.'

'I told you, I'm not an idiot. I've been assessing risk a long

time now. And you've been very clear on the subject,' she added
dryly.

'So—'

'So I'm not interested in your scruples,' said Natasha crisply.
'I'm interested in your heart. And your body. In that order. But
I will take what I can get.'

'Natasha!'

Shocked him, had she? Good!

She looked at the stars behind his shoulder and smiled wick-
edly. 'Interested?'

His answer was wordless. It stopped her breathing for a good
ninety seconds and was deeply rewarding.

Eventually he lifted his mouth from hers. 'You're crazy,' he
said into her hair, shaken.

'Maybe.' She took his hand and pulled him into the room
with its carvings and cushions and the big inviting bed, now
bathed in moonlight.

'And so am I.' But he went with her, unresisting.

She was breathless and laughing, even as she ached for him.
'You're a risk. I'm a risk-taker. I'd say we're made for each
other.'

They were trembling as much as each other as they tore at
unfamiliar clothes, hardly able to bear to leave off kissing as
they scrambled out of the scraps of cloth and tossed them away.

Natasha's skin was pale as gossamer in the moon shadow.
Kazim caught his breath. She reached for him, her heart in her
eyes...

And a small electronic ring tone shattered her world.

Kazim stopped as if he had been shot.

'What am I *doing?*'

He flung himself away from her, rifling through their fallen
garments in search of his phone. He found it and turned his back
on her.

'Yes? Oh, it's you, Tom.' He sounded crisp, wholly in command of himself. 'What? No, nothing important. Carry on.'

It cut Natasha to the heart. She would not have believed anything could hurt so much. Pulling the sheet across her nakedness,

she slipped off the other side of the bed and retreated to the darkest corner of the shadowed room.

Kazim did not waste words. 'Right. I'll be with you immediately.' He cut the connection and began to pull on his clothes, not looking round. 'Something's come up. Got to go.'

He did not, Natasha noted, say, 'I'll be back.' And she did not ask him. She already knew the answer.

She had fought for her life every way she knew how.

And lost.

CHAPTER TWELVE

IT FELT as if Natasha did not sleep. It felt as if she lay awake all night on the strange bed with unbearably tumbled sheets and hugged herself to stop from crying out with the pain of it. It felt as if she did not close her eyes.

But, of course, it was not true. When the first streaks of dawn clawed at the sky, they woke her. Her mouth felt like sandpaper and her head thumped with the residue of bad dreams. Lifting her head, Natasha saw that the filmy curtains were blowing about on either side of the French windows. She had forgotten to close them last night!

So Kazim could have come back into her room at any time, if he had wanted to.

'Conclusion,' said Natasha with irony, 'he didn't want to. End of story. The truth shall make you free.'

She groped her way out of bed and emptied a small bottle of water down her parched throat. Then she pulled an inelegant but cosy towelling robe round her and staggered out onto the terrace.

'What now?' she said aloud.

Kazim didn't want her. Or didn't want her enough.

'So I will go back to doing what I do best. Running my business and seeing my friends.' She shivered suddenly and pulled the robe tight up to her chin. 'And bridesmaiding is out from now on.'

The sea was indigo in the early-morning light. Sudden gusts of wind blew little sand eddies along the empty, perfect beach. It seemed as if there were no one else alive in the whole world.

And then she remembered. Kazim was to go and face his enemy in the desert this morning.

Suddenly all her clear-headed resolutions evaporated. All she

could think of was that she must see him, just once more. Talk
to him before he left. *Find him.*

She scrambled into the first shirt and trousers she could find,
and flung a desert robe over them against the early-morning cold.
Then she slipped down the outdoor staircase from the battlements into the main courtyard of the palace.

It too was empty. But she could hear a horse puffing and
hurrmphing somewhere close and there was an inviting smell of
coffee. She followed the scent to a smaller courtyard—and found
people at last.

Tom was there, looking strained, talking to two others in suits.
A man held the bridles of a couple of restive horses. Another
circulated with an engraved brass tray bearing thimble-sized han-
dleless cups and a thin-spouted pot. As soon as he saw her he
hurried up, offering it to her. The brew was both more fragrant
and more spiced than regular coffee, but Natasha still drank it
down gratefully.

'Kazim?' she asked.

But the man did not understand her and waved her towards
Tom.

It was unnecessary. He was already hurrying over.

'Kazim's gone,' he said without any of his usual politeness.
'He knew I would have advised against it. So he just went alone.
Before it was light.'

Natasha felt a cold hand tighten round her heart. 'Can we
catch him up?'

Tom looked at her with a new respect. 'We can try. Can you
ride?'

Natasha grimaced. 'If I have to.'

'You have to,' said Tom grimly. 'Kazim disabled the off-
roader.' He turned back to the other men. 'Okay, Martin, Ms
Lambert will come with me. Give her your hat and your horse.
You tell the Emir if we're not all back in two hours.'

He swung into the saddle with the ease of a man who had a
long line of cowboys in his ancestry. Natasha crammed the large
straw hat onto her tousled blonde head and climbed aboard

rather more inelegantly. But she didn't care. All that mattered was catching up with Kazim and telling him...

Well, telling him what? Goodbye? That he was an idiot? That she would probably wait for him for ever?

'All of the above,' muttered Natasha, furious with herself and Kazim in equal measure.

She was so furious, indeed, that she did not have time to feel nervous about her unaccustomed riding. She concentrated on staying close to Tom. He seemed to know where he was going and to be competent in getting there. She was concentrating so hard that she hardly took in the smooth, sculpted dunes, though they were like the dream landscape of the Thousand and One Nights. But she did draw a sharp breath when they breasted a slight rise and saw the tableau up above them.

Kazim sat on his mount like a statue. On the skyline, horse and man faced the blazing dawn. The pale robes blew in the morning wind. His shadow was a thin black dagger along the golden ground. If he was aware of Tom and Natasha, appearing out of the sunrise, he did not react. There were about twenty men around him, some on horses, some on foot, and a cascade of tents on the opposite slope.

Kazim ignored them all. He was utterly focused on the mounted figure directly in front of him.

They were eyeing each other like duellists, Natasha saw. The other man was shorter, more thickset and his horse was unhappy, tossing its head and sidling, snorting. He looked a thug, she thought, her heart suddenly in her mouth. She moaned.

Kazim's mount twitched its ears. Oh, heavens, had the sound carried in that still air? The hands on its bridle turned to iron suddenly. The horse stayed motionless.

Watching, Natasha thought: He is ready for anything. For all he looked so rock-steady, she knew instinctively that he would duck, or throw himself sideways or even leap completely out of the saddle, the moment the other man made a move.

She bit her lip until it bled. But she didn't make another sound.

Kazim's opponent pulled his horse back, rode away; then

turned and set his horse headlong, as if he wanted to ride the other man down. Kazim did not move until the very last moment, when he took his horse two steps out of the path of the oncoming charge. There was a diamond flash—a knife? A gun? Something flew high and landed on the sand, at a distance from the combatants.

Natasha's hand flew to her mouth, to keep in the scream of warning. Kazim, she saw, did not need any warning. All he needed was not to be distracted.

The horsemen began to circle each other. But this time they were clearly talking.

Natasha heard Tom give a great sigh. 'Thank God for that,' he said with fervour. 'All over bar the feasting. I hope you like goat.'

As she and Tom rode down into the encampment Kazim strode towards them. He did not look pleased.

'Oh-oh,' said Natasha. 'You've got that sheikh-of-all-I-survey look again. Will it be simpler if I just give you my mobile phone and you can throw it away now? Then you don't have to snarl at me first.'

The haughty profile got marginally more haughty. 'Be serious.'

'Well, that's what you usually do,' said Natasha, made frivolous by relief.

He helped her out of the saddle. 'What are you doing here?' he snapped as he did so. 'There was no guarantee what these guys would do. You could have got seriously hurt.'

Natasha was unimpressed. 'So could you.' She shook out her legs experimentally. 'Oh, boy, am I going to be stiff tonight.'

'Serves you right,' said Kazim unsympathetically. 'Have you any idea how I felt when I saw you sitting there on that damned horse?'

Natasha stopped fussing with her aching muscles. She straightened and looked him right in the eye. 'Oh, yes. I know exactly how you felt. Welcome to the club.'

He blinked twice. And said no more. But he watched her thoughtfully throughout the celebration.

Fortunately it was too early for goat. Instead, the men in the tents had prepared coffee and wonderful bread, fluffy as sponge cake, crisp as toast, which they served with warm, aromatic honey poured over the top.

They ate at a fairly brisk pace too.

'Everyone accepts that it's sensible to be out of the sun before it gets high,' murmured Tom in explanation. 'This won't go on as long as some feasts do.'

Natasha had no way of knowing whether he was right or not. She did know that when Kazim rose to depart all the muscles in her thighs and shoulders were just beginning to dread the journey back.

She made it—but only just. As all three of them cantered in through the outer gate she slumped forward on the horse's neck. It was sheer bliss not to have to pretend that she was in control of her horse any more.

Kazim gave a laugh—a heartless laugh in Natasha's view— and leaped lightly out of the saddle, throwing the reins to one of the men who came to meet them. Her horse stopped. Kazim opened his arms and either she fell off the horse or he dragged her into them. Natasha groaned—and her hat fell off.

'What you need is a bath,' said Kazim briskly. 'Soak those muscles before you seize up.'

He set off with her up the outer steps to her terrace.

'Put me down,' said Natasha, groggy but game. 'What will everyone think?'

He looked down at her, his eyes glinting with devilish laughter. 'Exactly what they thought when you chased after me into the desert this morning.'

Natasha digested that.

'Oh.'

They had reached the battlemented terrace. He set her gently on her feet.

'Why did you?'

Suddenly, astonishingly, she was shy. 'You know why,' she mumbled and looked away.

'Indulge me,' he said. He stroked a tendril of dusty blonde hair lovingly. 'Give me the words.'

Natasha met his eyes at last. This, she thought, this is important. I have to tell him the exact truth.

She said painfully, 'When you are in danger I want to be with you.'

Kazim took her hand then, and pressed it against his heart. She felt the steady beat of his blood under her palm, through the thin cotton. It was as familiar as her own pulse.

'You are,' he said simply. 'Always, I think.'

The look in his eyes made her head swim.

'Bath,' he said. 'Or you won't be able to walk tomorrow.'

She was disappointed, but she knew he was right. 'All right. I won't be long…'

But it seemed that he had no intention of leaving her to soak on her own. He drew a hot bath for her, added drops of oil that smelled of lime blossom, and then helped her out of her dusty gear and into the scented water. Natasha sank back with a sigh of total bliss and closed her eyes.

'So where do we go from here?' asked Kazim, seated companionably on the end of the bath.

She opened her eyes. 'Go?'

'Is it fair to put you through this every time some extremist decides he can use me to make a point?' he mused aloud.

Her heart sank. She did not answer.

'No,' he said, answering himself. 'But then I shall be going through it too, as you pointed out this morning.'

Natasha's eyes flew to his face.

'I'm a great believer in equality in marriage,' he told her. 'Particularly equality of anxiety.'

She ignored the teasing tone and fixed on the only word that made sense. *'Marriage?'*

He pursed his lips. 'Oh, I think so. If a thing's worth doing, it's worth doing properly.'’

She was floundering, absolutely wrong-footed. 'But we haven't even… I mean, last night you left…'

His eyes laughed at her openly. 'Quite. And I'm still certain I can't live without you. That has to be love, wouldn't you say?'

'I—I—'

'Unless it's not me at all. Maybe you're just mesmerised by the romance of the east,' he mused naughtily. 'I've read that women like to be flung across the crupper and carried off into the desert.' He shook his head sadly. 'Maybe that is all I am to you? The fulfilment of a fantasy? To be tossed aside after a few weeks?'

Natasha might be overwhelmed with love and lust, but she was an independent woman and she had the power balance of her future relationship with this man to consider. She sat bolt upright, sloshing water around freely, including on the skirts of his robe.

'You need to update your reading,' she told him crisply.

He laughed and kissed her so hard that his entire robe was soaked and clinging to him by the time he had finished.

'Now are you going to marry me?'

Natasha emerged panting and aroused, but she valiantly hung onto some semblance of sanity. 'I'll think about it.'

'What's to think about?'

'As you pointed out, I rode after you into the desert,' she observed. 'It's all a bit one sided, so far. You're such a believer in equality. You want to marry me? Prove it.'

And she sank back in the bath and lowered her eyelids in what she hoped was a suitably alluring challenge.

Kazim stood up. And Natasha's blood began to beat a whole lot faster. But instead of stripping off his robe and leaping into the scented water with her, he felt carefully in the wet pocket and pulled out something that looked like a small bird's nest.

She stared, uncomprehending.

'I told you you were with me this morning,' said Kazim, with a smile that reached all the way from his eyes into his heart.

A couple of limp rose petals drifted down into the water. She looked and looked at them. And slowly realisation dawned.

'My bridesmaid's headdress,' said Natasha, amazed. 'You kept it.'

'I thought it was all I was ever going to have,' he said simply. 'Is that proof enough?'

Their eyes met in perfect understanding. Natasha had not realised it was possible to be this happy. She drew a long, shaky breath and got out of the bath.

Kazim put his arms round her then, and held her as if he would never let her go.

'More than enough,' she said. And took off his robe at last.

MILLS & BOON®

Live the emotion

Tender romance™

HER ITALIAN BOSS'S AGENDA *by Lucy Gordon*

(The Rinucci Brothers)

Olympia Lincoln is so relieved when her new assistant shows up – she sets him to work immediately. What she doesn't realise is that he's actually Primo Rinucci, her new Italian boss! Primo can't resist playing along – this way he can get really close to the beautiful Olympia…!

A BRIDE WORTH WAITING FOR *by Caroline Anderson*

Annie Shaw believes her boyfriend, Michael Harding, died in a brutal attack nine years ago. But he's actually been forced to live undercover… Now Michael is free to pick up his life and reveal himself to the woman he loves. He can only hope that Annie will fall in love with the man he has become…

A FATHER IN THE MAKING *by Ally Blake*

After waiting so long to hear from the Gaspers, Laura thought they couldn't care less about her – or her daughter, Chloe. So when Ryan Gasper turned up at her Outback home she was understandably suspicious. Ryan's career – his life – was back in the city, but something about Laura made him want to stay…

THE WEDDING SURPRISE *by Trish Wylie*

Desperate to save her father's business, Caitlin Rourke enters a reality TV contest with the prize money in mind! To win she must convince her family that she's marrying a stranger – but as she gets to know her fake fiancé, Aiden Flynn, she finds it impossible to keep her feelings for him a secret…!

On sale 6th January 2006

Available at most branches of WHSmith, Tesco, ASDA, Borders, Eason, Sainsbury's and most bookshops

Visit www.millsandboon.co.uk

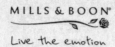

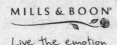

FREE!

4 Books
and a surprise gift!

We would like to take this opportunity to thank you for reading this Mills & Boon® book by offering you the chance to take FOUR more specially selected titles from the Tender Romance™ series absolutely FREE! We're also making this offer to introduce you to the benefits of the Reader Service™—

- ★ **FREE home delivery**
- ★ **FREE gifts and competitions**
- ★ **FREE monthly Newsletter**
- ★ **Exclusive Reader Service offers**
- ★ **Books available before they're in the shops**

Accepting these FREE books and gift places you under no obligation to buy, you may cancel at any time, even after receiving your free shipment. Simply complete your details below and return the entire page to the address below. You don't even need a stamp!

YES! Please send me 4 free Tender Romance books and a surprise gift. I understand that unless you hear from me, I will receive 6 superb new titles every month for just £2.75 each, postage and packing free. I am under no obligation to purchase any books and may cancel my subscription at any time. The free books and gift will be mine to keep in any case.

N5ZEF

Ms/Mrs/Miss/Mr ....Initials ....
BLOCK CAPITALS PLEASE

Surname ....

Address ....

....

....Postcode ....

Send this whole page to:
UK: FREEPOST CN81, Croydon, CR9 3WZ